Also by Bob Stockton

- *Counting Coup:*
  The Odyssey of Captain Tom Adams
- *Fighting Bob*
- *Listening To Ghosts*
- *Stories from the U.S. Navy:*
  I. A Suicide in the Mediterranean

A Man Who Lost His Wife

and Other Stories

Bob Stockton

First published by Dog Ear Publishing
4010 W. 86th Street, Ste H
Indianapolis, IN 46268
www.dogearpublishing.net

ISBN: 978-1-4575-3669-4

This book is printed on acid-free paper.

Printed in the United States of America

This book is dedicated to the memory of
Frank R. Stockton

CONTENTS

I.

Previously Unpublished Stories

A Man Who Lost His Wife

The man approached the table and asked whether the seat next to mine was taken. He smelled like he had spent the afternoon drinking somewhere.

I couldn't fault him for that. I'd had a couple myself before the dinner was scheduled to be served.

"No," I replied. "Have a seat and join us for dinner."

I had recently flown to a city in the southwest to attend the annual conference of a charitable association of retired servicemen. The dinner was the President's Reception Dinner, a catered welcoming affair in which the association president greeted the attendees and their wives and laid out the schedule of events for the four-day conference.

"Thanks. Hey, the bar is still open. Join me in a cocktail before dinner?"

I thought about it for a moment.

"What the hell, don't mind if I do. Vodka and tonic for me."

"Vodka tonic. Got it. Be right back."

The man turned and walked unsteadily to the hotel bar, ordered the drinks, and returned to the table. I was impressed with the man's dexterity once he had the drinks in hand. He didn't spill a drop on his return trip.

"Here ya go, vodka and tonic for you and a double Jack for me, one for each leg. Don't want to wobble when I walk."

I nodded.

"Words to live by. Thanks for the drink. Here's to health."

"Thanks, and back at ya. Name's Harry. Ya sure I'm not taking your wife's seat?"

I indicated to Harry that I was attending the conference alone.

"Stay where you are, Harry, I'm here by myself."

"Ah, well, okay then. Leave the wife home, did ya? Or don't she like these meetings? I like 'em myself, get together with old friends every year, have a good time, ya know?"

I nodded and gave Harry a friendly smile.

"No. I'm divorced. I'm usually traveling solo for these affairs."

It was as if Harry hadn't heard my reply. He continued his monologue in a loud voice.

"And did ya see the set of cans on that bartender? Is she hot stuff, or what? Man, oh man, what a honey!"

I was beginning to second-guess my decision to invite Harry to join me at the table. He was obviously drunk, and his crude remark had been loud enough for the dinner guests several tables away to hear. The small talk between the other couples at the tables nearest ours ceased, and all eyes focused on Harry...and me. Icy stares would be a more accurate description of the attention that the two of us were getting from the married guests at those tables. I turned to Harry and made a moderating downward gesture with both hands.

"Harry, everyone heard your last remark. This probably isn't the ideal place for talk like that."

"Oh geez! Was I talkin' that loud? Damn. I sure am sorry, didn't know that everybody could hear me. Not used to comin' to these things by myself. My wife would always tell me when I was gettin' too loud and all, but she ain't with me no more. Lost her two years back."

I wasn't exactly sure what Harry meant by "lost her" and was pretty sure that I didn't want to hear Harry's explanation. I decided to take the conversation along a different tack.

"Harry, have you signed up for any of the scheduled tours?"

"What? Oh the tours. Yep, signed up for two of 'em, the Alamo and that canal boat tour that goes right through downtown. They oughta both be pretty good. Ya know once I see the Alamo, I can say that I been to where ol' Davy Crockett was born and where he died. He was born near Johnson City, Tennessee, ya know. They got his ma and pa's dirt-floor cabin all preserved over there. Not much to it, either."

"That is something, isn't it? I don't think that I've ever met anyone who has been to both places."

"Uh huh. Got a whole state park there with RV hookups and all. Real nice the way they fixed it up.

"Gonna take that downtown barge tour, too. Goes right through the city, past restaurants and shops and all. She woulda really liked that one, ya know."

Harry paused, obviously trying to control his emotions. His eyes were filling with tears. He took a deep breath, pulled out a handkerchief, and blew his nose. It was obvious to me that when Harry had spoken of losing his wife, she had died…and fate had dictated that I was to be the guy who was to hear Harry's story. I decided to be a good listener. We were, after all, brothers in military background.

"I'm sorry. It must be hard to lose someone that close to you."

"Had a modular home built just below Las Cruces after I retired. Real close to Holloman and Fort Bliss. We'd go to the commissary over there at Bliss once a week and over to the base hospital to get our prescriptions filled.

Sometimes we'd do all that on a Tuesday 'cause the NCO club had bingo on Tuesday nights and she was just about as lucky as you could get at that damn game. That's what they called her over there, ya know, Lucky. Kind of like her nickname, it was."

Harry's voice had been reduced to a near whisper. He blew his nose again and continued.

"We got back from our Tuesday bingo—she'd won a couple of small jackpots, ya know, and we was both kind of tired and went right to bed. Come one thirty in the next morning, she wakes me up and says, 'I can't breathe good.'

"Well, ya know she had heart problems, and I asked her did she take her heart medicine that day, and she said that yes she had."

The retelling of the events surrounding his wife's death had helped Harry regain control of his emotional state.

"Well, I said get dressed and we'll hustle up to the hospital in Las Cruces and see what's the problem. She said okay, and we got into the pickup and headed over to the hospital.

"We got there, and I let her off at the emergency room door and went to park the truck. Found a spot and I come back into the emergency room and I don't see her. I go up to the nurse at the desk and tell her who I am and ask where is my wife?

"Well, the nurse says that they took her in back and to wait around and the doctor will be out in a little while to talk to me. I ask if I can go back there with her, and she says not just yet, they are pretty busy back there. She says it won't be long and the doctor will be out to talk to me.

"Well, I'm not real happy 'bout all that, but I figure that my pissin' and moanin' about all of it ain't gonna help anything, so I go over and sit down to wait for the doc to come out tell me what the scoop is."

I was a bit ashamed for having tried to manipulate the conversation earlier for my own selfish reasons. After two years had passed, Harry was obviously still unable to cope with the loss of his wife.

"Harry, I'm empty and it's my turn. How about a refill?"

"Well yeah, just a beer this time, Coors if they got it. I'm about topped off on the Jack."

"Done."

I walked over to the hotel bar, purchased two bottles of Coors, returned to the table, and set one down in front of Harry.

"So Harry, was it very long before the ER doctor came out to talk to you?"

Harry gently touched my bottle of Coors with his bottle.

"Thanks, good health and cheers. Took the doc 'bout half an hour before he comes out and says that she's having a bad time with her heart failure and was she on some kind of medicine pill called furside or somethin' like that? I showed him a list of the medicines that she took, and he nodded and said yeah it was on the list. Then he said that they was gonna admit her and try to get some of the water out of her.

"She had been tellin' me of late how her ankles and everything was swellin' up and that it was gettin' hard for her to walk. Said the next time we was over to Bliss that she wanted to make an appointment with a doc over there to see what they could do."

"So they admitted your wife to the hospital?"

"Yep. Doc said that they wasn't any reason to be worried, that I should head home and get some sleep and by the time I got back to the hospital the next day she'd be ready to go home, prob'ly with some new medicines that would help her heart more.

"I wasn't real hot on leavin', but the doc said that they'd be busy with her for a while and I couldn't go back there while they was workin' on her and the best thing I could do was get some rest in my own bed.

"Said they'd call me if anything was to happen."

"So you went home to get some shut-eye, yes?"

"Went home but didn't get much shut-eye. Phone rang about an hour after I got home. Caller ID showed it was the hospital. I answered it, and some nurse from the intensive care unit called, said I was to come back to the hospital, that the doctor wanted to talk to me. I asked her what was goin' on, and she said the doctor would talk to me when I got there.

"I figured that maybe they needed some more information about the Medicare or the Tricare, so I got up and went back over to the hospital to give them whatever they needed to have and to get my wife to take her home."

Harry paused, drained the bottle of beer, and wiped his eyes with his handkerchief.

"Got over there, and they take me into an office where some chief doctor of somethin' is, and they tell me that my dear wife has died. I said, 'How can that be?'

"They said they couldn't get the water out of her lungs fast enough, that her heart wasn't workin' good enough to get the water out."

Harry paused again to get control of his emotions.

"She drowned in her own water. We'd been married thirty-seven years."

Harry looked down at his dinner, which had been served while we were talking.

"Ya know, I don't feel real hungry now. I'm gonna head up to my room. You goin' on the Alamo tour tomorrow?"

I nodded.

"Sure am, Harry. Ought to be a pretty interesting bit of Texas history."

"Well, maybe we can get together and take the tour together, seein' as we're both flyin' solo."

I nodded again and smiled.

"Who could pass up the opportunity to tour the Alamo with a guy who has seen where Davy Crockett was born?"

*   *   *

A Conversation at a Book Signing

"This one book here, *Listening to Ghosts*, is it about ghosts on ships?"

"No, sir. Well, not exactly. The title refers to the people that you have served with or known in the past. You can remember their names and some circumstances where you and that person knew each other."

"I don't get it."

"Let me try to explain it this way: there are people that you have interacted with in the past that have affected you in such a way that you can still see them in your mind's eye and maybe even can hear their voice. That's what I meant when I came up with the title for this book."

"I don't know anyone like that."

"Hm. Well, as we are in a military exchange store, I assume that you are retired military. Which branch of service?"

"Army. I'm a retired sergeant first class, but I don't remember anyone from all that."

"Oh. Well what about your drill instructor from your basic training?"

"Williams! That bastard!"

"There you have it."

*　　*　　*

The Bandit

Jimmy Romeo, better known as "the Bandit," had fallen on hard times. Jimmy was an old-time light heavyweight fighter, veteran of nearly two hundred professional fights, two of which he had split with the legendary light heavyweight Archie Moore. He had made hundreds of thousands of dollars during his career, and what his manager hadn't stolen went for brandy and beautiful women, which eventually left him broke and on the street with only his meager Social Security pension. Bob Morgan hired Bandit now and then for odd jobs and to occasionally invite an unruly patron to leave the premises of his saloon. Other than that, the notorious Jimmy "Bandit" Romeo, once the scourge of west coast boxing, now addled, scarred, and gnarled from more than twenty years of taking and giving punches, was left to indulge his taste for cheap brandy by cadging drinks from customers at the bar. The bar patrons didn't mind. In fact, they enjoyed being seen in the company of the legendary west coast warrior for only the price of a glass of bar brandy.

Jimmy Romeo got up from his stool at the end of the bar and walked over to me.

"Did I hear my name mentioned? Perhaps an offer of a brandy or two may have been in the conversation?"

Bandit's appearance was exactly as I remembered him: a full head of snow-white hair, slightly cauliflowered ears, flattened nose, scarring above both watery brown eyes. He was dressed in an old army field jacket, T-shirt, shabby and frayed jeans, and worn sneakers.

I turned to the man and extended my right hand. Bandit took my hand in his own huge, knuckle-scarred paw. We shook hands briefly.

"Jimmy, you probably don't remember me. I was home-ported here a couple of years ago and we had a few drinks together then. It's good to see you again. I'd be honored to buy you a brandy or two."

"Indeed I do recall, my young friend. No man is an island. I remember that you and one of the ladies from the theater next door were friends."

The bartender, Smitty, returned with two shot glasses filled with bar brandy. Bandit took one in his giant paw and drained it.

"Ah. Thank you, my friend. No man is an island. When one of us passes, ask not for whom the bell tolls; it tolls for thee."

Bandit lifted the second glass of brandy, raised it in a half salute as a gesture of gratitude, and quickly drank it down.

"Ah. Thank you, young friend. I'd return the favor, but I'm needed next door. Bob has some errands for me to run. Perhaps next time."

I smiled and clapped Bandit on his muscled arm.

"Next time will be just fine, Jimmy. See you then."

Jimmy "Bandit" Romeo smiled, nodded, and exited the bar.

I turned to the bartender and raised my empty glass to signal for another rum and coke.

"Smitty, I see he's still saying that 'bell tolls' thing. What's that all about?"

Smitty shook his head.

"Dunno. One of the winos that comes in here on Social Security check day who was a professor or something said it comes from an old English poem. Like about how we are all connected, or something. Jimmy may have had a lot of his brains knocked about, but he heard that somewhere once and it must mean something to him. I heard someone say not too long ago that one of his fights resulted in his opponent dying, but Bob says that there is nothing in the record books that shows anything like that. It's a mystery, and I guess we'll never know for sure. I don't think that by now, even Jimmy knows what it means."

"Well, Smitty, it just could be that he's not as punchy as everyone makes him out to be. I haven't seen him in a couple of years, but he did remember me and he remembered that I was running with Anita next door."

Smitty shook his head.

"Nah, he's had his head scrambled once too often. I mean, who wouldn't? The guy had close to two hundred pro fights. God only knows how many amateur fights and brawls he's had. There are times that he just zones out and just sits at the bar and talks to himself."

I nodded in agreement.

"Yeah, well, it's not like he's a threat or a bother, or anything. I was at the bar one night before you were working here when Bob asked Jimmy to give a guy the bum's rush. The guy was all drunk and was being nasty around Franny. Bob was hot about it and told Jimmy to work the guy over a bit on the way out. Jimmy wouldn't do it. He told Bob that he'd help the guy out the door but that he didn't want to hurt anyone. I didn't know who Jimmy was at the time and thought that he was just a big gentle guy.

"Anyway, Jimmy went up to the guy and told him that he was making a disturbance and that the owner would like him to 'please leave.' That's exactly what he said, 'please leave.'

"The guy wasn't a sailor; he was dressed too well—suit and tie, the whole nine yards. I had the impression that he was waiting for one of the chorus girls next door to finish the last show and that he couldn't hold his booze very well.

"Anyway, the guy stood up and got in Jimmy's face, called him an old geezer or something like that, and told Jimmy to go sit down and mind his own business.

"Jimmy pleaded with the guy. 'I don't want trouble; just go on and leave.' I mean, he was almost begging the guy not to provoke him."

Smitty nodded.

"So did the guy leave after that?"

I shook my head.

"Nope. I guess the guy figured that Jimmy was some kind of pushover, with Jimmy being so polite and all. Then the drunk guy made a fatal mistake."

Smitty was grinning from ear to ear.

"I can see it coming."

"Yep. The guy figured that Jimmy was just some old wino, so he got up as if to leave, turned around to give Jimmy a shove with his...let's see...yeah. With his right hand.

"That shove didn't even get to Jimmy's shoulder before...wham! Jimmy uncorked a heart punch with his left, and the guy flew back about ten feet and landed right on his ass. Took the guy about a minute to get his breath back. Jimmy then went over to the guy and helped him up and told the guy that he didn't want to do that and now was he ready to leave?

"The guy looked at the Bandit like he couldn't believe what just happened. I don't know if he still couldn't get his breath or he was just too scared to talk. He was just standing there all wobbly, staring at Jimmy. The Bandit raised that big left paw of his and made a fist. The guy by this time was beginning to get the message and just nodded , turned around, and wobbled out the door.

"Bob and the people at his table were laughing. They all said that the guy must have not been on F Street before 'cause everyone on F Street knew the Bandit. Bob tried to hand Jimmy what looked to me like a twenty, but Jimmy, as broke as he was, wouldn't take it. He told Bob that Bob and Franny were his friends and that they did plenty for him as it was and that he was just helping his friends."

*　　*　　*

Naomi Lukas

I had planned to write a story about my erstwhile lover, the deceitful, lying alcoholic Naomi Lukas, but as you can see, I've thought better of it.

*   *   *

The Dream

Most of what he remembered of his nightly dreams were usually surreal fragments, bits and pieces of some hypnagogic landscape where nothing made any real sense and where ghost-like others would appear, make a cryptic remark or two, and disappear into the fog of his unconscious. Those landscapes were always vaguely familiar—familiar enough so he knew that he had been there before but could not quite put his finger on why he was there now and whom he was supposed to see. The dreams always flashed through his subliminal mind and vanished slowly into the haze of awakening, never to be rediscovered, leaving him feeling strangely unfulfilled for not being able to remember the dreams in their entirety.

This dream was different in that he could remember all of it. When he awoke the following morning, the dream was waiting for him in his conscious mind, ready to be resurrected and dissected in an attempt to discover whatever epiphany the dream was meant to convey.

*   *   *

It was the house at the beach in the Old Cove neighborhood. She was getting items ready for some sort of garage sale. She had placed a circular clothing rack—the type that you see in T.J. Maxx or Marshalls that displays the markdown items—on the driveway just in front of the garage door. Hanging on the rack among the other sale items were his baseball hoodie and his old chief petty officer blouse, the one with the gold hash marks.

She must have made a mistake, he thought, and brought the two items back into the house.

He showed her the hoodie and blouse. "You made a mistake," he said. "We're not selling these."

She said nothing in response, just gave him the look that she had been so fond of sharing with him of late.

"How much do you want for your jacket on the rack?" he asked.

She looked at him. "Ten dollars, no excuses."

"You mean no exceptions," he corrected.

She gave him that look again.

He walked outside and noticed that there were three packages by the front doorstep. He knew that he and his wife hadn't been anywhere recently and was slightly irritated that the UPS guy hadn't made an effort to get them to him. He looked at the labels and saw that they were addressed to someone who lived in the beach town five miles away.

"UPS is usually better than this," he said aloud and wondered how he was going to get the parcels to their rightful owners.

He started to walk into the garage to tell her about the packages when he noticed a man approaching. The man was dressed in a dark suit and tie and looked very uncomfortable in the suit. He was a working man and was wearing the suit for this encounter only.

"I'm from the laundry," the man said, "and I understand that you and she have had a baby, so I wanted to come and tell you about our laundry service."

The man in the suit had an odd, strained smile on his face.

"You have the wrong address," he replied to the man in the suit. "I used to own and operate a dry cleaning plant, did all the spotting and ran the machines, bagged and put the orders on the conveyor, all that. Had to hire pressers, though. I couldn't press."

The man seemed uninterested in his reply.

He looked down the street toward the light-green house diagonally across from the street's intersection. A man was walking up the drive toward the front door. He waved to the man, and the man responded with a desultory flick of his hand.

He walked into the garage to tell her about the man at the green house.

"I thought that it was Clarence, but it wasn't. It was Jimmy—you know, the light-skinned kid with the bright blue eyes. The one that slashed our tires that time."

She said nothing in response, just gave him that damned look again.

*   *   *

He sat up and looked at the clock. The time was a quarter to eight.

"I better let the dog out," he said aloud.

*   *   *

Abbott and Costello

"Good morning. Did you write this book, *Listening to Ghosts*?"

"Yes, sir. I wrote all of the books you see here on the table."

"Neat. This is my son Curtis. He is an avid reader. I'm Phil."

"Pleased to meet you, Curtis, and you as well, Phil. Do you have any questions for me regarding my books?"

"What is *Listening to Ghosts* about?"

"It is an autobiography."

"Oh! I like those. What about you, Curtis?"

"Sure do, Dad."

"Well, then we ought to get it. Whose autobiography is it?"

"Dad, it's an *auto*biography."

"I heard him. The book is about who?"

Sigh.

* * *

Bar Michi

"The only thing that the Japs here like about Americans is their money."

The winter of 1966 in Japan was cold and wet, the skies a dismal and depressing gray. It seemed to me that the cheerless weather had influenced the residents of Yokosuka similarly, as they all affected a rude and resentful attitude toward Americans, which meant that the rest and recreation stand-down from our bombing campaign over North Vietnam would most likely be neither restful nor recreational.

My friend and fellow squadron crewman George Sturgis was an old Asia hand. He was explaining to me why he thought that Yokosuka was the worst liberty port in all of Asia for a sailor.

"I'll say one thing for 'em, they don't make no bones about it. They just want your money and don't care if you know it. 'Bout all you can do here is grab a steak dinner at the Club Alliance, have your liquor ration card punched, change your scrip for Yen, and grab a hotsie bath and special massage at the New York Bathhouse up on the hill."

Scrip, or Monopoly money was more formally known as MPC. While in Japan, all American military were paid in scrip instead of dollars. The local bars and restaurants were prohibited from accepting the dollar substitute, and consequently, when sailors went ashore, they went to the Club Alliance, a military exchange located off base, to exchange their scrip for Japanese yen. American dollars were expressly forbidden because of the Status of Forces agreement between Japan and the United States to discourage black marketeering.

American dollars if traded on the local economy brought a much higher exchange rate than the 360-yen-to-one-dollar official exchange.

We had been to a few bars in Thieves Alley and purchased a few Asahi beers at high prices, and I had even bought one "hostess" a drink at one of the bars. The drink was basically sugar water and incredibly overpriced. Once the drink was paid for, my hostess spent all her time conversing in Japanese with another, equally short, bowlegged and rude bar girl at the next table.

"See what I mean? They think they're better than we are. Ain't no wonder there's so many Hiroshima jokes floatin' around the Alley. At least in the P.I. and Hong Kong, nuthin's off the table. You can fall in love—or maybe it's just heat—in the P.I. but not so here. Here they want as much as they can get and give nothing in return. Don't like 'em. Never have."

I nodded in agreement. George had brought home his point about liberty in a Japanese port.

"What do we do next? Are all the bars like this?"

"They are in the Alley. Down at the end is a Fleet Reserve Association Branch for the ships and sailors home-ported here. Mostly old-timer retirees who went native and married one of the bar girls here go to the Fleet. They retired and never left. Last time I was here, there was even an old chief bos'n's mate that was at Pearl Harbor in forty-one. Came here for duty on the harbor tugs, married one of 'em from the Alley, and they live in one of those apartments that have paper walls and a benjo ditch instead of a toilet. Big sumo wrestling fan like all the retired round eyes that stayed over here. When the matches are on, they all go over to the bar at the Fleet Reserve and argue over which tub of lard is the best. Never seen anything like it."

I smiled at Sturgis's description of the Yokosuka Fleet Reserve Branch.

"I wonder if the chief and his wife celebrate Pearl Harbor Day?"

Sturgis laughed.

"Don't know, but I'll bet it makes for some lively conversation at their apartment that day and most likely for a few days after."

Sturgis and I had seen enough of Thieves Alley. He offered a suggestion.

"Well, what say we grab a cab and head on up the hill to the New York for a hotsie bath?"

"I don't know, George. What exactly is this 'special massage' that you've been talking about?"

"You go in there and buy the hotsie bath, and this girl in her skivvies comes out and takes you in. You get undressed, and she wraps you in a towel and takes you for a steam. After the steam, she gets a stool and scrubs you down, balls and all. Then she rinses and dries you off and gives you a massage. After the massage, she asks if you want the special massage. That's how they make their money—you tip 'em for the special massage, see? The bathhouse gets the cost of the hotsie bath, and the girl gets the tip. The sailors always want the special."

Sturgis grinned.

"Last time I was here, I went through twice. Never felt so clean."

I smiled and nodded.

"I reckon I know what a special massage is if you went through twice."

"Yep. Tip her a couple thousand yen, she takes off her bra, grabs the lotion bottle, and goes to town. What say we head up that way?"

"Well, as thrilling as it sounds, I'll pass this time, George. I think I'll just look around a bit."

"Suit yerself. I'll see you back on board."

We left Thieves Alley and walked to the main boulevard. George hailed a cab, waved goodbye, and rode off. I headed up toward what looked to be a tunnel, mindful of the fact that traffic patterns in Japan are the exact opposite of those in the States. It would be all too easy to look left while starting to cross the street and get hit by a car coming from one's right.

As I walked along the street, I passed a number of small shops, which lined the sidewalk that led to a train depot located at the mouth of the tunnel. Among the shops was a small establishment which displayed a sign that was written in both Japanese and English: Bar Michi.

I walked in to find a small bar—perhaps seven or eight stools. A young girl was behind the bar, which had one Japanese customer, a middle-aged man who was already seated and slurping some sort of soup from a large bowl.

The young girl gave me a cheerful greeting in near-perfect English. She wasn't dressed like the girls working in Thieves Alley; she was attired in a skirt and blouse and wore a sweater and knee socks to help ward off the winter chill.

"Hello, sir. May I help you?"

The Bar Michi was obviously not a sailor bar but rather a quiet, cozy place frequented by a few Japanese customers to have some sake and pass the time of day. Occasionally, a Navy man such as myself would drop in but wouldn't stay long when they discovered that the bar was nothing more than a neighborhood place for the commuters from the train to stop for refreshment and catch up on their friendship with the family that owned the establishment.

"I'd like a whiskey and water, please. It's a bit chilly outside."

"Yes, sir. I have VO, Canadian Club, and Suntory. Which do you prefer?"

"Let me try the Suntory, miss. With water."

"*Hai, dozo.* 'Tory and *mizu.* If you are chilled from outside, perhaps a hot bowl of soba, yes?"

"Soba?"

"Yes, sir. Hot noodles in a soup."

"You know, that does sound good. How much for the drink and the soup?"

"Five hundred yen, *dozo.*"

"Really! Is that all? That is very reasonable. I'll have the soba and the whiskey, please."

"*Hai, aregato, ne?*"

The young girl gave an oh-so-slight bow with her head and shoulders and then walked through the curtained doorway behind the bar and spoke rapidly in Japanese. Having placed the soba order with someone in the back room, she returned to the bar and mixed my drink.

"Here you are, sir. 'Tory and *mizu.* That means Suntory whiskey and water."

There must have been a soup pot already on in the back, as my soba order was ready within a few minutes and was served by a stout fiftyish woman with rather thick glasses.

"This is Mama-san. She and Papa-san own the bar. My name is Kimiko. I am the older daughter."

I returned the shoulder-and-head bow that the two women gave me. Kimiko giggled.

"I am pleased to meet you, and I like your bar and restaurant very much. My name is Bob."

Kimiko nodded slightly, indicating that she understood. She then turned and spoke to Mama-san in rapid
Japanese. The only word that I could recognize was my
name. When Kimiko was finished, Mama-san gave me a
broad grin and nodded her head.

"*Hai*. Bob-san. Bob-san."

Mama-san looked at Kimiko and, while smiling,
spoke to her daughter in Japanese.

"Mama-san English is not what you say good. She
asks me to tell you welcome to the Bar Michi. She also tells
you that this is not like the Alley places. They are thieves
and what?...Cutthroats? Is that the right way?"

I thought for a moment and then replied,

"Yes, I believe that she's right about that. I would say
that she has accurately described the goings-on down in
the Alley. Please tell Mama-san that I am delighted to meet
her and if it doesn't make her customers unhappy, I'd like
to come here more often."

Kimiko turned and translated my response to her
mother, who smiled broadly, said something in return, and
scurried into the back room.

"Mama-san says we are pleased to have you visit with
us many times and she would like you to meet our family.
We have rooms in the back of store."

I had been busy devouring the bowl of hot, delicious
soba noodles. Kimiko's remark caught me a bit off guard.

"I... ahem...the soup is very hot, you know. Anyway,
I'd be pleased to meet your family, Kimiko. Your hospital-
ity reminds me of home."

Kimiko giggled again and turned toward the behind-
the-bar entrance to what must have been the family's living
quarters. As the name of the establishment was Michi, I

assumed that it was the family surname but decided to wait for introductions.

First through the curtains was a very old and stooped man with closely cropped hair. He was dressed in sandals, khaki trousers, and a sport shirt worn outside his pants. The old man was nearly toothless and had to be at least twenty years older than Mama-san. At first I thought that he was the grandfather, but during the subsequent family introductions, I learned that he was indeed Mama-san's husband and the father of her three children.

The oldest child was a son. Everyone called him George for some reason. George worked for a Japanese banking firm and was the family driver, as he and he alone knew how to operate the family Toyota. Next came Kimiko, who, along with her mother, ran the day-to-day family business. Kaziko, the youngest daughter, was a high school student. At the time of our introduction, she was still wearing the plaid skirt, white blouse, and knee socks that female schoolchildren in Japan were required to wear.

* * *

During the course of our stand-down period in Yoko-suka, I visited Bar Michi nearly every day and got to know the family quite well. Papa-san, old, toothless, and unable to speak clearly enough for anyone outside his immediate family to understand, relied on Kimiko to convey his meaning to the outside world. While she was interpreting his remarks to me, the old man would nod his head vigorously and laugh "ha-ha-ah-ah-ah" all the while. I couldn't help but like him; he reminded me of my great-grandfather from Slovakia, whose speech I also couldn't understand.

Papa-San was not Japanese, as Kimiko would reveal to me during one of my visits. He was Chinese, originally from Nanking, and had survived the slaughter in that city by the Japanese Army in 1936. He had been captured and brought to Japan for slave labor in the shipyard in Yokosuka and survived on scraps of food and vermin-infested rice that his captors had given him while he worked eighteen hours a day as a laborer. When the Americans had rebuilt the shipyard, he had stayed on as a laborer, eventually saving enough money to marry and open Bar Michi.

Papa and I became fast friends over the next few years. He would share his stories with me through his daughter, and I would buy him the occasional whiskey, being careful not to buy too many, lest I incur the wrath of Mama-san.

*   *   *

"Bob-san, Mama has died since you were last here."

Spring of 1968. It had been some nine months since my last visit to Bar Michi. Mama-san's son, George, shared the sad news with me as I entered the bar.

"George, I am so sorry. How are Papa and the girls doing?"

"Papa is sad, says he doesn't want to go on much further. My father is eighty, you know."

"I knew he was getting on in years. Tell him I'm thinking of him. What about the girls?"

"Kimmie is okay, I think. Kazi is having a very hard time without her mother."

I nodded.

"Please, George, if there is anything that I can do—"

Just then, Papa came through the curtain into the bar. I guess that he heard George talking with someone. When he saw it was me, he came shuffling over to the bar, head nodding, wringing his hands and talking excitedly to me. I couldn't understand and turned to George for help in translating what Papa was saying to me. I assumed that he was telling me about Mama.

George listened respectfully, then turned to me with Papa's translation.

"Papa says that it is a sign that you have come here at this time, that you are part of our family and that he wants you to come to the ceremony day after tomorrow. He is very excited that you are here."

"Ceremony? What ceremony is that?"

"When a Buddhist dies, there are memorial ceremonies at different intervals that happen at the dead person's house, where an altar has been built. We have some rooms here in back of the store, but we also have a house about ten miles from here. The day after tomorrow is the forty-ninth-day memorial ceremony. Papa says it is good that you've come here, that it is a sign and he wishes that you would come with us to the ceremony."

"I'm certain that I can arrange that. Tell Papa that of course I will go to honor Mama the day after tomorrow. Is there anything I need to know? You know I'm not Buddhist, and I don't want to offend anyone, least of all Papa...and Mama."

George nodded.

"Wear your dark uniform or a dark suit. You ride with us in the Toyota. When we get to the house, remove your shoes before going inside. There will be a cushion in the back of the room for you to sit. Our Japanese family will sit in the front, very close to Mama's altar. There will be prayers and incense and some flowers by Mama's picture at the altar. When the service finishes, each person leaves something at the altar, usually yen, in accordance with their closeness to Mama. If you wish, you may put something by the altar after everyone has done. What you put there is up to you, maybe one or two thousand yen."

"George, how do you and the rest of your family feel about my going to Mama's ceremony?"

George smiled.

"We would be quite pleased."

I looked at Papa and extended my hand.

"Please tell Papa that I am very grateful for his invitation and am honored to go."

Papa didn't need a translation. He clasped my hand with both of his thin, gnarled ones and held it close to his breast. His eyes watering, he nodded his head rapidly.

"Ha-ha-ah-ah-ah."

* * *

"I'll be gone this Saturday to visit friends in Yokosuka. Is there anything on the conference schedule?"

I was attending a pharmaceutical business meeting at the Four Seasons hotel in Tokyo in the spring of 1994.

"No, sir, nothing on the schedule until Monday. We'll be at Daichi all day that day."

"Good. See you then."

I grabbed a cab at the hotel entrance and rode to the train station, where, with the help of several amused Tokyo residents, I bought a round-trip ticket to Yokosuka from a vending apparatus that looked like a pachinko machine and followed directions to the proper platform on the lower level. The ride was made longer by one stop after another to take on and drop off passengers along the way. I was amazed at the American commercialization of the train advertisements. Apparently, the Japanese liked Subway and MacDonald's while Americans were flocking in droves to sushi bars and Japanese steakhouses in the States from coast to coast.

Finally, we arrived at the end of the line. I could feel the excitement build. I was sure that after twenty-six years, Papa had gone to his reward, but what of George, Kimmie, and Kazi? Were they married? Were there children? I thought of the various reunion scenarios as I walked the two-block distance to Bar Michi.

I approached the storefront that I was certain was for Bar Michi. The sign had been taken down and replaced with a sign written only in Japanese. I walked inside to inquire about the whereabouts of my Japanese family.

"Bar Michi? Bar Michi? Is this Bar Michi?"

The young man looked up from his reading with a puzzled look on his face.

"Is this where Bar Michi was? Do you know Kimiko and Kaziko? George?"

The man shook his head and looked back at his reading.

"Don't know. Don't speak good English."

I visited every store on the block, to no avail. One older woman who spoke some English remembered the family. She said that they had been gone for more than ten years and didn't know where they had gone or what had happened to them.

*　　*　　*

Negotiation

"Well, I don't know. I'm twenty-three. How old did you say you were?"

"I won't lie to you. I'm half past sixty."

"I don't know. I've never been to bed with someone who is sixty."

"Time is of the essence."

*   *   *

The New Cadet

Sonny had just turned eleven when his mother broke the news.

"You have too much free time on your hands after school, which is getting you into trouble. You have failed three of your subjects at Willey School, and you have been playing hooky about as often as you have been at school. We're making a change starting with the September school year."

Sonny wondered if this change to which his mother referred had anything to do with her taking on a second job typing county court trial transcripts from the Dictaphone equipment in the evenings after dinner.

"You will attend summer school this summer, and after school, you will go to your aunt Anne's house until I get home from work. Next Tuesday, you and I have an appointment to meet with Colonel Balzer, who is the commandant of cadets at Bordentown Military Institute, where you will begin the seventh grade as a day student."

Sonny couldn't believe what he was hearing. Summer school meant no vacation trip to Wildwood by the Sea for two weeks of boardwalk rides, restaurants, and beaches. And BMI? Military school? Anything but that. Anything.

"There is no use complaining about it. I have made the appointment, and we're going to take the bus next Tuesday. We have a ten o'clock appointment."

*   *   *

"Cadet, you have rather large shoes to fill. Your cousin Richard was an outstanding cadet-scholar. He was destined to become the battalion commander, had he not died so suddenly."

It was the first day of the 1951 school year, and Sonny was officially a member of the cadet corps. The dismal situation in which he found himself could only be exacerbated by comparisons to an older cousin whom he had met only once when he was not even five years old and who apparently had been a model cadet before he had died from some mysterious blood disease.

And the daily schedule! His seventh grade school day began sharply at 0745 hours, with battalion parade formation, where uniform inspection by the cadet company commanders was held. Shined shoes and belt buckle, pressed pants, clean shirt with necktie properly tucked in the shirt front, and garrison cap properly worn was the standard to which each cadet was held. Any infraction of the dress code would result in "penalty tours," two hours of close order drill each afternoon held after school hours. After inspection, the plan of the day was broadcast to the cadets by the public address system loudspeaker. The battalion was then dismissed and the cadets went to their respective classes. Before the war had begun in 1950, there had been a raising of the flag and playing of the national anthem during parade formation, but as Colonel Balzer and Major Agnew, Professor of Military Science and Tactics, explained, the colors were never struck during time of war because it would signal defeat to the enemy. Sonny wondered exactly which enemy they meant. His immediate enemy was Sergeant First Class Conradi, a retired Army infantry sergeant who was on the BMI staff as drill instructor and made his life miserable during drill period.

It didn't take very long for Sonny to rank among the leaders in penalty-tour hours amassed for either a uniform infraction or for a tardy slip for being late to class. Another lower school cadet—lower school was the designation for the youngest cadets attending seventh and eighth grades—Sam La Doux had an unofficial contest going with Sonny to see who could amass the most penalty tours. La Doux usually was in the lead. He was another day student from Wrightstown who was continually gigged for wrinkled uniforms, shirttail out, scuffed shoes, insubordination in ranks (he was constantly chattering during Sergeant Conradi's drill periods), and tardiness. La Doux was never where he was supposed to be at the appointed time.

In spite of all the new surroundings, military-like regulations, and demanding academics, Sonny eventually decided that although he didn't love attending the military school, he didn't hate it either. He actually enjoyed the drill periods overseen by the ever-present, ever-scolding Sergeant Conradi. He became quite proficient in guiding right, manual of arms, and other aspects of formation drill that taught the cadets the discipline of teamwork. He was even promised a squad leader position if he could eliminate his penalty tours and bring his grades up from the overall C– average that he was carrying. He liked the idea of being a squad leader but just couldn't seem to get running on all cylinders simultaneously. One week would bring penalty tours for a haircut infraction or some uniform discrepancy; the next week, it would be tardiness to a class. Always something! If he would only focus more on his uniform and being on time, on getting his math and introductory German grades up from their near-failing level, he'd be a much better and much happier cadet, said his instructors.

* * *

The 0745 formation at the school in Bordentown was some eight miles from Sonny's Trenton home, which meant that he would have to be up, dressed in the uniform of the day, and out of the house by 0700 to ride the intrastate Public Service bus at 0710. The bus ran from Trenton with a stop in front of the military academy after a trip of some twenty minutes; if there weren't too many passenger stops along the route, he had barely enough time to get to the parade ground, take a quick inventory of his uniform, swipe the tops of his shoes on the back of his pant legs, and assume his place in the company formation. The struggle to get to formation and squared away on time never seemed to get better. What Sonny really needed was ten more minutes before formation to get settled in, but the bus schedule was what it was and his family didn't own a car, as his mother and grandmother didn't know how to drive.

One very cold morning early in January, Sonny left his Trenton house at 0655 and walked to the corner to wait for the bus that carried him to school. He had been waiting for about five minutes when a gray four-door Pontiac pulled up to the curb where he was waiting. The driver was dressed in the uniform of a United States Air Force master sergeant. The sergeant leaned over and rolled down the passenger-side window.

"Kind of cold out there, isn't it, cadet? Would you like a ride down to BMI? That's where you're headed, right?"

"Yes, sir. That's where I'm headed. Are you going that way?"

"It's only a little out of my way. If you want a lift, get on in."

"Thank you, sir. I appreciate the ride."

"Not at all, cadet. Look, I go this way every morning during the week at this time. It would be no trouble to give you a ride to school."

Sonny wasted no time in answering.

"Thank you, sir. That would be quite helpful to me. I'm always on the edge of being late for morning formation with the bus schedule being what it is."

The sergeant smiled.

"Well then, it's settled. I go by this corner every morning at 0700 on my way to McGuire Air Force Base. If you are out there, I'll give you a lift. After all, those of us who are in uniform have to stick together, don't we?"

Sonny couldn't have been happier. A ride every morning meant that he'd'd be able to arrive a few minutes earlier and prepare for morning formation. It also meant that he would keep the bus fare for a snack at the school canteen during morning break.

"Yes, sir. Thank you, sir, we sure do."

The sergeant smiled again and offered his hand for a handshake.

"Look, if we are going to ride to Bordentown every morning, there's no need for the 'sir' business. That gets old fast. My first name is Al, or if you are not comfortable with that, you can call me Sergeant. I'd prefer Al, but it's up to you."

Sonny returned the handshake.

"Well, if it's okay, I'll call you Al. Everyone calls me Sonny."

"Roger that, Sonny. Glad to meet you. What grade are you attending at BMI?"

"Seventh, sir...er, Al."

Sonny was a bit uncomfortable referring to the sergeant by his first name, but if it meant a free ride, he'd darn well get used to it. Besides, it was good to share the ride time in the mornings with an older male, as he lived in a house with his mother and grandmother. His father had left the home when Sonny was still a small child.

*   *   *

"Did you know that Sonny has been getting in a car every morning with some strange man?"

Sonny's grandmother was informing his mother of his transportation option one morning in mid-April.

"What are you talking about, Mother? He takes the Public Service bus every morning."

"No, he doesn't. I've been watching from my bedroom every morning for the past week. He goes to the corner, and a car picks him up and takes him to God only knows where. I'll bet he's off getting into trouble somewhere."

"Just a minute, Mother. If he's doing this, there must be some explanation for it. He could be getting a ride with another schoolmate whose father takes him every morning."

His grandmother shook her head.

"There ain't nobody else in that car but the driver. God only knows how long this has been going on. And what's he doing with the bus money you give him?"

"Alright, Mother, that's enough. I'll take care of this. Is he home yet?"

"Up in his room. He's supposed to be doing his homework, but he's probably listening to that portable radio he got for Christmas."

Sonny's mother left the room, went up the stairs to the second floor, and walked along the hallway to the door to the attic bedroom.

"Are you up there?"

"Yeah, Mom."

"I'm coming up. I have something that I want to discuss with you."

"Yes, ma'am. Come on up."

His mother walked up the steps to the converted attic bedroom. Sonny was lying on the bed with his open history textbook.

"Your grandmother tells me that you've been getting into a car every morning instead of taking the bus to school. Is that true?"

"Yes, ma'am."

"Where do you go, and who is this person who picks you up in the morning?"

"I go to school. He gives me a ride to school every morning so I won't be late for morning formation."

"I want to know who he is and why he's giving you a ride."

"He's a U.S. Air Force master sergeant stationed at McGuire in Wrightstown. He's been in the Air Force for twenty-two years! It's on his way, pretty much, and he gives me a ride. He likes to say that guys in uniform have to look out for each other. He's a good guy, he really is, Mom. Tells me a lot about how the military works, and stuff."

Sonny's mother thought about the situation for a moment. On the one hand, she knew that her son would benefit from some sort of father figure-type relationship that had been missing in his life since her divorce from his father. On the other hand, she knew nothing about the man other than his military occupation.

"While we're on the subject," she said, "what have you been doing with the bus money I give you?"

"Take the bus home, Mom."

"What about the fare to school? Where does that go?"

"I use it for a snack during mid-morning break period."

His mother nodded.

"Well, here's what's going to happen. You may continue to get a ride with this soldier—"

"Airman, Mom."

"Airman, fine. You may continue to ride with him in the morning, and tomorrow morning, I'm going to go to the corner with you to meet this sol...airman."

A look of horror crossed her son's face.

"Mom, do you have to? He's a real good guy, honest. He tells me a lot about the Air Force. It's really neat, the kind of planes he's worked on and everything. He even has a pilot's license."

"No arguments. If you want to ride with this man, I want to meet him. If you don't want me to, then it's back on the Public Service bus for you."

* * *

The sergeant rolled down the passenger-side window and smiled.

"My guess is that you are Sonny's mother and you'd like to know who I am."

"How do you do? Yes, Sonny hasn't said anything about this to me, and I understand that you have been giving him a ride to school every morning."

"Yes, ma'am. Master Sergeant Al Flanagan. How do you do? I gave him a ride one cold day last winter, and seeing as it is on my way and it's nice to have a bit of company for part of the ride down to McGuire, I offered to give your son a lift in the mornings. I had no idea that he didn't tell you about it, and I can understand your concern."

"You're sure he's not a bother?"

"Oh, no, ma'am. Your boy is a fine youngster. He is no trouble at all."

"Can I give you something for gas?"

"No, I wouldn't think of it. As I say, it's good to have some company for part of the ride."

Sonny's mother nodded in the affirmative. She had made her decision.

"Alright then, if he is no bother. Thank you very much, Sergeant."

"My pleasure, ma'am."

Sonny's mother smiled and returned to the house.

"Well, what did you find out?"

"It's fine, mother. The man is a career Air Force sergeant who goes to work that way in the mornings and gives Sonny a lift to school. His grades have been improving lately, and I think it's good for him to have a man's influence in his life."

"Just the same, I don't like it."

"Alright, Mother. You don't approve. We'll leave it at that."

*   *   *

"So How was the plane ride? How high up were you?"

It was a warm July day. Sonny was hanging around the McClellan Avenue playground with his neighborhood best friend, Del Strong.

Sonny paused briefly, then answered his friend Del.

"It was okay. We didn't go very high, maybe two thousand feet."

"Shoot, that's all? What the hell kind of airplane is it?"

"Piper Cub, the kind with the passenger seat right behind the pilot's seat. No doors on it. I had to make sure that my seat belt was strapped real tight."

"No doors? Neat! When is he gonna take you up again? You think he'd give me a ride too?"

"No, because I ain't goin' up with him again."

"Ain't goin' up with him again? Why not?"

"Because he's a queer."

"What? Are you sure? He couldn't be a queer, he's an Air Force sergeant!"

"I don't care if he's a general. He's a queer."

"You mean he's queer like Crazy Walt, who gives kids a quarter if they let him feel them up in the movies on Saturday afternoon? *That* kind of queer?"

"Yes, Del. That kind of queer. Let's drop it."

"Sonny, that can't be right. How do you know that?"

Sonny heaved an exasperated sigh.

"Because when we were in the car after the plane ride, he grabbed my prick and tried to kiss me. Said he'd give me ten dollars if I let him blow me."

"Jeez o man! A queer Air Force sergeant! What'd you do?"

"You don't see me throwing any money around, do you? What the hell do you think I did? I got out of the car and thumbed a ride home. I told him if he bothered with me anymore, I was gonna call the cops."

"Wow! What did he do then?"

"He just laughed and drove away. Ain't seen him since, and don't want to either."

"Jeez o man! A queer Air Force sergeant. What did your mom say?"

"Ain't told her. I don't want to have to listen to my grandmother about it. Next school year, if she asks, I'll just say he was transferred.

Now can we stop talkin' about it?"

* * *

Mama Lee

In its heyday, the Sportsman's Saloon, located on an out-of-the-way street in an unremarkable strip mall near the river, was a novelty. The saloon was the very first sports bar in the city and was packed full nearly every night. Little League coaches would bring their young charges in on the weekends after a game for French fries and soda. The Sportsman's Burger, a grilled half-pound ground-beef burger prepared to order and garnished with a thick slice of sweet onion, ripe tomato, and iceberg lettuce on a toasted bun, was the talk of the town. Jumbo satellite dishes fed every sports event of the day to the huge projection screen on the east wall and to the half dozen or so smaller televisions strategically lining the other three walls. A peanut machine dispensed heavily salted free roasted peanuts that were still in the shells. Customers were encouraged to just throw the empty shells on the saloon floor, from where they would be swept up at closing time by a less-than-enthusiastic wait staff. The Sportsman's Saloon was a fun place to spend an afternoon or evening. Everyone came dressed in their favorite team's football jersey and cheered enthusiastically for their alma mater or their professional sports team of choice. Eventually, other businessmen in the food and beverage industry began to take notice, and after a year or two, the city landscape was dotted with sports bars, which began to affect the business at the Sportsman's Saloon. The original owner, alleged to have been in some financial distress, sold the Saloon to a retired Navy chief petty officer who successfully ran the business for several years before deciding to sell to Lucille.

It was a quiet Saturday evening, even for the once famous and now largely forgotten Sportsman's Saloon.

Lucille, the new owner, had, after taking ownership of the establishment, promptly committed the unforgivable sin of installing a jukebox on the premises.

A jukebox! Why in the world would anyone want to have a jukebox in a sports bar? Doesn't this new owner understand that the patrons of a sports bar are there to watch sports, not to play tunes on a damned jukebox? Next thing you know, she'll be putting doilies in all the booth tables and...and...featuring karaoke on Saturday night!

Is nothing sacred?

Well, no...not exactly. Karaoke was scheduled for Wednesday nights, and the regulars began to desert the Sportsman's Saloon in droves. I stayed with the Wednesday happy hours longer than most of the saloon regulars, but eventually, the caterwauling and screeching of amateur song-birds belting out their favorite tunes in the wrong tempo and horribly off key was too much. I began to frequent the café on the adjacent street regularly, paying only an occasional visit to the Sportsman's Saloon. Call me sentimental, but that saloon had been a part of my happy-hour evenings for nearly ten years. It was hard for me to completely walk away.

I didn't feel much like cooking that quiet Saturday evening, so I decided to head over to the Sportsman's Saloon for a beer and a burger. I hadn't been there in several months and had heard reports from some of the past regulars that the saloon had undergone a change in clientele. The karaoke crowd and trivia buffs had replaced the sports aficionados, and the jukebox was loaded with row after row of country-and-western ditties that bemoaned some relationship gone wrong or a loved one who was shot in bed by a jealous paramour...or cuckold...or both. Hell, I don't know.

I must have arrived early, as there were only three people in the bar: Lucille, the owner, and an older couple, Buddy and Marilee McDonald. I said hello to the McDonalds and greeted Lucille as I sat down at the west end of the wraparound bar.

"Coors Light and a Sportsman's Burger, please, Lucille. Kind of quiet here tonight, isn't it?"

"We don't have any entertainment scheduled for tonight. What you see is what you get.

How you want your burger?"

"Medium. Loaded, but hold the mayo."

"Got it. Be right back with your beer."

Lucille walked over to the kitchen window and handed my burger order to Timmy, the short-order cook, then retrieved a bottle of Coors Light and brought it to me.

"Cold mug?"

"Yeah, that'd be nice. Thanks."

"Dr. Bob, how in the world are you? We haven't seen you in a cat's age."

Marilee McDonald, known to everyone as Mama Lee, was speaking to me.

"Hey, Mama Lee and Buddy. I'm okay. You know, so far so good."

The McDonalds were originally from Opelika, and both were Auburn alumni. Mama Lee had taught second grade at the local elementary school for more than forty years until retiring a year earlier. Everyone said that there wasn't anyone who lived in this part of town, young or old, who hadn't been in her second-grade class at one time or another. Buddy was retired from a sales position with a local electrical supply company. They had lived in the neighborhood for the better part of fifty years.

"Well, Dr. Bob, what are you doing with yourself these days now that you have sold your dry-cleaner plant?"

Mama Lee was updating her file on me. Everyone also said that if you wanted to know anything about anyone in this part of town, just ask Mama Lee. She always knew what everyone was doing.

"Working with a contract company on a contract for Novartis Pharma. Keeps me out of town about three weeks out of every four."

"Well, Dr. Bob, you're working too hard. You need to find a job where you can be closer to home."

"Don't I know it! I'll think about it at the end of this contract next year."

Buddy had a thought on the subject.

"Well, you ought to be getting close to retiring, I would think."

"Five more years, Buddy, then I'm hanging 'em up for good."

The door to the saloon opened. A man walked up to the bar and took a stool about four places down from Buddy and Mama Lee.

"Draft and a burger. I want it rare."

Lucille took the order without greeting the man, poured a Budweiser from the tap, placed it in front of the man, and delivered the food order to Timmy, then walked over to my spot at the opposite end of the bar and whispered to me,

"If there's trouble with this biker, I'll need your help."

"Me? Me? Why me?"

"Because Buddy's too old and Timmy's in the kitchen, too far away. Just grab a pool cue and hit him with the fat end."

"At least Timmy has knives. Have you looked at this guy? He looks like he wipes his ass with sandpaper."

"May not be anything going down, Doc. Just be ready in case."

"This is what I get for being too lazy to cook."

"What was that?"

"Never mind. I'll do what I can. Just don't aggravate him."

The biker had a request.

"If you two are done talkin' over there, I'll take another beer."

Lucille turned and went over to pour another beer.

I figured that if I was going to get killed in a barroom brawl, I'd better take measure of the guy that would be punching my lights out. He was of medium height, unshaven, stockily built, and well-muscled. His hair looked like it hadn't seen soap and water in months and was apparently slicked back with a mixture of bear grease and motor oil. His dungaree pants were torn, and from his wide leather skull-buckled belt was strung a chain, which secured his wallet in his back pocket. There was some sort of club patch on the back of his motorcycle jacket. His face appeared to be safety-wired in a scowl.

I wanted to be anywhere but where I was at this moment. I just knew there was going to be trouble.

And then an angel of mercy appeared. The angel had the voice of a no-nonsense second-grade teacher.

"Billy Holcomb, is that you sitting over there with that look on your face?"

The biker turned to look in the direction of the voice and, while turning, recognized the voice of Mrs. McDonald, his second-grade teacher. His countenance immediately changed.

"Oh, ah...yes, ma'am, Miz McDonald. It sure is, Miz McDonald."

"Well, Billy. How are you? Are you staying out of trouble?"

"Um...well, um, yes, ma'am, pretty much."

"That's good. And how is your mother?"

"She's fine, ma'am. Living up in St. Marys."

"Well, when you see her, give her my regard. Are you working somewhere?"

"Yes, ma'am. I'm a motorcycle mechanic with a shop down St. Augustine way."

"Billy Holcomb, your mother would be very disappointed if she knew that you went around in public dressed like that. People do not know you as well as I do, and they will get the wrong impression when they see you. You need to work harder on your hygiene habits."

"Um, yes, ma'am, that's right. I sure will think about doing just that."

"Alright then, Billy. It's good to see you again, and please remember me to your mother."

Mama Lee turned to me and spoke.

"Dr. Bob, Billy here was one of the best-behaved students that I ever taught. You don't have to worry about him making any trouble."

She turned to the biker.

"That's right, isn't it, Billy?"

"Oh, yes, ma'am. Right as rain. Miss, will you please wrap my food to go?" he said to Lucille.

"Miz McDonald, ma'am, I have to be going. It sure was good to see you again."

"Alright, Billy. You behave yourself."

"Yes, ma'am, I sure will."

The biker took his food, paid the tab, and left.

Like I said, there wasn't anyone who lived in this part of town, young or old, who hadn't been in Mrs. McDonald's second-grade class at one time or another.

*   *   *

Tucker's Note

Arthur "Tucker" Soden died of congestive heart disease. Tucker was my mother's friend and companion for the dozen or so years prior to his death in 1975. His death was the only time that I ever saw my mother cry.

At some point during his life, something occurred that profoundly affected Tucker. Whether it was his past divorce, his weak heart, or his business reversals is not known to me. Among my mother's possessions when she died in 1980 was this note written by Tucker on a page torn from a telephone address book. I recently came across the note in a catch-all drawer in my kitchen and have carefully reconstructed Tucker's thoughts from those faded and tattered pieces of the original. In his memory, his note is presented here.

* * *

Have you ever noticed how often fate will play the coward's game; how sometimes she will lie in wait for a man, until he is sailing along serenely, confident in his thoughts for the future, only to slip up behind him when he is least prepared, and lay him by the heel with some sly trick in which he may not even recognize her hand for the instant? If you have not, think upon it now. Watch for it the next time hard luck overtakes you. Or, better still, look back into the past and consider the blows which she has dealt you. Could you see her coming then? Can you see her coming now?

Of course you could not!

* * *

II.

Stories Adapted from
Listening to Ghosts

Dying Alone

My house on South Broad Street was one half of the typical attached two-story, attic-topped homes with sitting porch that were built in the first decade following the turn of the century. Running along the side of the house was a narrow walkway, which passed two small windows that allowed access to the two coal bins in the house's cellar and continued on, ending at the gate, which guarded the entrance to the small yard in the back of the house. Once or twice during the late autumn and winter, a coal delivery truck would back up onto the curb in front of my house, temporarily blocking the sidewalk, and park as closely to the coal bin windows as possible. The driver would then deploy the long hinged collapsible chute from the truck bed along the walkway and position it into the open coal bin windows, one window at a time, to deliver the coal, which fueled the furnace, which in turn furnished steam to the iron radiators in each room that provided heating during the winter. The amount of steam entering a specific radiator could be controlled by a wheeled valve on the steam line, which could regulate the amount of steam entering the iron radiators. If one wanted to change the setting to allow either more or less steam into the unit, one picked up a hand towel and turned the small horizontal wheel atop the valve stem accordingly. I had lost track of the number of times I had burned my hand on that damned wheel.

The house had none of those new air-conditioning window units to combat the stifling summer heat—they were much too expensive. Floor fans were placed in each room to circulate the warm air in the rooms. Each year in the early autumn, my grandmother would summon uncle Mack to replace the window screens with the storm windows that would help to insulate the house during the cold winter months. Uncle Mack would reverse the process in the spring, replacing the storm windows with their screened counterparts.

The combined wages of my mother and grandmother were not enough to keep the household heated, pay the electric bill, provide groceries, and keep a rapidly growing boy in clothes. The decision was made to take in a boarder whose rent money would help with expenses.

There was one problem. Located on the second floor were the three bedrooms and the house's only bathroom. If a boarder were to be taken in—only female boarders would be considered—there would be no room for me. Where was I to sleep?

Uncle Mack provided the answer. My grandmother summoned her brother-in-law once again, and he promptly arrived with his tool bag (Uncle Mack was a building contractor), measured the unheated attic, ordered drywall from a local building-supply company, walled off a section of the attic for storage, and converted the rest of the space into a bedroom. The new attic bedroom was to remain unheated. During the winter months, blankets, a heavy quilt, and an electric space heater were provided. The heater plugged into a two-receptacle outlet located by the attic stairwell. There was a night light plugged into the second outlet to illuminate the steep makeshift stairs that Uncle Mack had built. In the summer months, the heater was replaced by a floor fan, which attempted to capture and circulate the cooler night air across the makeshift bedroom. The open screened attic windows were no barrier to the noisy traffic passing by the house at night, which at first kept me awake. Unable to sleep, I would sit up in bed, watching the automobiles pass by along Broad Street, quizzing myself about the identity of the cars by recognizing the shape of their taillights.

The sleeping accommodation problem being solved, my family went to work to find a suitable boarder for the spare second-floor bedroom. As luck would have it, one of my grandmother's former neighbors, Edna, happened to be looking for accommodations at the time and was invited to rent the spare bedroom.

Edna was an unmarried fortyish woman whom everyone called Hoppy. Although she was older than Mom, Hoppy and my mother had been friends as children. She was the perfect boarder. Hoppy helped with the housework, would get dinner started, as she was always the first to arrive home from work, and presumably paid her rent on time.

Hoppy worked on the production line at the local Westinghouse plant. She would get up every morning at five o'clock, get ready for work, and catch the bus across the street from the house to get to the manufacturing plant, which was located across town. Her production line shift was from seven o'clock to three thirty, the day shift. Eventually, she became one of the family, sort of like an aunt rather than a boarder—an aunt whose direct family connection was a bit blurred, but an aunt nonetheless.

Hoppy had a gentleman friend, Bill Cooper, whom she had first met before the war. Bill had been drafted by the Army and had been sent to North Africa as a meteorologist. He had returned a sergeant in 1945, been discharged, and gone to work for the local weather bureau. Bill was a married man who had been separated from his wife for many years. He kept putting Hoppy off about marriage, saying that his wife wouldn't give him a divorce, but he was sure that she would come around "soon." Hoppy was apparently willing—or perhaps resigned—to wait for the unspecified day when Bill Cooper's wife would grant him his freedom. The whisper among the adults in my family was that Bill Cooper was in no hurry to press the issue. After all, there was surely the specter of alimony that would emerge as a result of a divorce, and Hoppy was cleaning Bill's apartment every week and providing him with companionship. What was the rush? Bill Cooper was perfectly content to put Hoppy off, promising her that "someday soon," his estranged wife would grant the divorce that Hoppy so fervently hoped for. Hoppy, for her part, felt that Bill was probably her last chance for marriage and went along with the charade.

Saturday was date night for Bill and Hoppy. Bill would arrive at the house impeccably dressed in a gabardine suit and straw hat. The family would gather to sit in the living room, waiting for Hoppy to make the grand entrance from her upstairs bedroom. She was always just a bit late, which caused Bill, a fastidious man, some discomfort. Finally the clop, clop, clop of Hoppy's platform shoes echoing on the wooden stairs would announce her impending arrival just before she came grandly into view. Hoppy would always be dressed as if the two were attending the Mayor's Inaugural Ball or some such prestigious event. Off they would go in Bill's car into the early evening for dinner and an evening's escape from the humdrum of their daily life.

My grandmother couldn't stand Bill. Her opinion was that Bill Cooper was "too light for heavy work and too heavy for light work." She always suspected him of dropping

Hoppy off after their date and "sneaking drinks in a saloon somewhere," an allegation that was confirmed years later while I was home on leave from the Navy. I had stopped into a downtown watering hole one Saturday night for a nightcap or two, and lo and behold, there was Bill Cooper putting a few "behind his necktie." Bill had dropped Hoppy off after their Saturday date and had stopped in for a few scotches. I was now a submarine sailor stationed in Norfolk, and Bill and I had a few drinks and chatted amiably until closing time. It was to be the last time that I would see Bill Cooper alive.

*   *   *

Several years after my grandmother died in 1960, the government decided to close the Trenton Weather Bureau, leaving Bill unemployed. He eventually found work in a furniture store, selling furniture from the showroom floor.

Bill and Hoppy never did marry. He died suddenly of a heart attack while shoveling snow in front of his apartment one winter morning. Hoppy never recovered. Not much of a drinker before Bill Cooper's death, she began to drink heavily. My mother would get rid of the bottles that Hoppy would hide around the house, only to have Hoppy buy more, hiding the bottles in the toilet tank and other places where she thought they wouldn't be found. My mother often found Hoppy passed out on the stairway to the second floor, too drunk and disoriented to get to her bedroom.

Several years after Bill Cooper died, Hoppy succumbed, alone and unmarried, in the total throes of alcoholism.

*   *   *

Modern Twentieth-Century Living

Suddenly, inexplicably, he remembered his friend Donnie's breathless announcement from more than sixty years past, which opened the synaptic floodgate that until now had restrained the memories from his old neighborhood.

"The drugstore has a real TV! It's on top of the phone booth."

Television was the coming thing. I had seen the sets in the display windows of the downtown department stores while shopping with my mother. There was always a crowd gathered outside those windows, which exhibited the different sets for sale at what seemed to my mother to be unaffordable prices. Both table model sets and the more expensive console floor models with the twelve-inch cathode ray tubes set in rich mahogany surroundings were on display, all available for purchase: Philco, Zenith, Dumont, RCA, and Magnavox, all right there in the store windows and ready to be delivered to the buyer's home—delivery, antenna, and installation extra, of course. For a few dollars more, a remote-controlled antenna motor could be purchased that would turn the receiving antenna toward the more distant stations in Newark and New York City so vague and snowy images could be viewed.

Six channels! Modern twentieth-century living! The summer of 1949 was going to be like no other summer that I could remember.

*   *   *

The television of which Donnie had spoken was located in the drugstore at the end of the block. It was a table-model Philco with a six-inch diagonal cathode ray tube that delivered a grainy black-and-white picture and was, as Donnie had so accurately described, perched precariously on the top of the pay phone booth in the corner at the end of what used to be the lunch counter. The store proprietors were Messrs. Garb and Lopatin—Harry and Bill. Both were pharmacists. The store had so many over-the-counter items for sale that customers had to crab-walk to get to the rear of the store where the prescriptions were compounded. Much to the dismay of the neighborhood kids and of Betty, the lunch counter waitress/short order cook, Harry and Bill had converted the lunch counter in the store to a merchandise display area. That old lunch counter had offered standard drugstore lunch sandwich fare: tuna salad on toast, grilled ham and cheese sandwiches—the ham sliced so thin that my mother said the customer could "read a newspaper through it"—burgers, hot dogs, and so forth while the soda fountain had created some of the best ice cream sodas, sundaes, and banana splits in town. I suppose that the drugstore patrons viewed the demise of this neighborhood oasis as progress. Donnie and I viewed it as the closing of ice cream heaven.

Betty viewed it as a visit to the unemployment office.

At any rate, Harry and Bill were good neighbors who never objected when a pack of kids would descend upon the store on Tuesday nights to watch Milton Berle's *Texaco Star Theater* on that old Philco set.

*   *   *

The neighborhood had a distinctive middle-class aura at one end and a more blue-collar, lunch-pail atmosphere at the other, which was scarcely three blocks distant. I lived directly next door to the truck dealership, which sold and repaired all manner of International Harvester trucks. The next block housed a Sunoco filling station, which sat next to a lumberyard. Not two blocks from my house in the opposite direction was a tidy, neatly landscaped Methodist church, which was situated next to the Professor Markowitz Studio of Piano, which in turn was next to the dental office of Doctor Teddy Vine (reputed to have been a hotshot third baseman in his high school days at Trenton Central) and a small department store that had noisy, creaky wooden floors. None of the neighborhood kids from the lunch-pail side of the neighborhood could shoplift from that store, as those old wooden floors made too much noise. Mister Berg, the owner of the store, or his nerdy son Bertram would hear them come in and descend upon the kids with a sarcastic "May I help you?" followed by a "No browsing. You kids get back to your own block and make trouble down there."

*　　*　　*

Bertha and Mabel

Bertha and Mabel lived two houses down from Harry and Bill's drugstore. They were retired schoolteachers in their sixties and hadn't changed their style of dress since the Great Depression. Their house was set back from the sidewalk, always dark and guarded by a chain-link fence. Bertha, who was the dominant sister, decided one day that she would learn to drive, and damned if she didn't succeed. She returned home one afternoon in a drab gray four-year-old Chevy sedan. I would see them every Sunday afternoon, each with hair pulled back in a severe bun, wearing no makeup and drab neck-to-ankle dresses, Bertha at the wheel, driving somewhere for a Sunday outing. They kept to themselves, especially Mabel. It was as if their home was an island of virtue surrounded by a world gone mad. There would be none of those godless television things in their home, no, sir!

Bertha and Mabel shared my family's telephone party line, which was mostly a pain in the backside but at times could be quite funny. I will never forget the time that I had attempted to call a classmate from military school who lived in Maryland. Bertha had kept picking up her receiver, which would then abort my connection.

"I'm trying to call someone in Maryland," I said, using my very best official tone.

"Well, that's a shame," Bertha had replied, "because you've only gotten as far as down the street."

*   *   *

Adventures in Boy-Scouting

Heading west on Broad Street brought one to the intersection of Buchanan Avenue and Broad Street. The Broad Street Park Methodist Church and rectory were situated on the corner. It was in the cellar of that church that the local Boy Scout troop met every week. My mother thought it would be good for me to be a Scout, and so I was drafted into the troop, not really wanting to do all that "nature stuff," but they did show cartoons there occasionally, and the uniform looked pretty spiffy, so in I went. The scout troop spent a lot of time tying knots and talking about Indians, and of course there was the obligatory two weeks at Camp Pahaquarra, the Boy Scout camp up at the Delaware Water Gap, that had to be endured. The troop was bivouacked in a series of huts that had canvas flaps for walls that were deployed only when it rained. It was two weeks of pure hell as far as I was concerned. Even though more than sixty years had passed, I remember three distinct things from my only camp year there: (1) poison sumac followed by liberal applications of calamine lotion, (2) a blood blister on the tip of my left middle finger, received when I had incorrectly fed the camp donkey a slice of apple (apparently, it liked the finger as well), and (3) Buster Graham, a kid from my troop who loved to light his farts. I left scouting after that first season, never even having made Tenderfoot.

Nothing in the above paragraph should be construed as impugning the Boy Scout creed. On the one hand, great leaders, war heroes, captains of industry, and athletes have emerged from their ranks. On the other hand, scouting has also spawned any number of insurance salesmen and politicians as well.

* * *

The Bus Driver Who Was Also a Father

The passage of years following my father's sudden death, though not affording me total closure, has at least given me a measure of acceptance and understanding of the complexities of that flawed human being who had been my father. My father—I called him Pop—had been as unsuited for fatherhood as any man could be. What Pop had really wanted were sons with whom he could pal around while visiting several of his favorite watering holes, regaling them with tales of his past conquests, and daughters to wait on him during the infrequent times when he was not sitting on a barstool in some saloon somewhere. Pop was simply not suited to parenting small children. That took up too much of his free time and required much too much responsible behavior.

While most fathers' legacies to their sons were designed to guide those sons toward successful and rewarding lives, Pop's legacy to me (aside from a late-blooming case of corneal disease) was a series of one-liners. On proper saloon etiquette: "If you can drink and drink with grace, you'll be welcome in any tavern." On finance: "It's the loan company's fault. They should have known I could never pay the loan back." On philosophy: "Booze is the only answer." During the summers when I had no school and Pop was in between jobs, I would accompany Pop while he "ran a few errands," which generally meant one or two stops to drop off his shirts at the laundry or to pay the light bill with a check written by his wife so he couldn't cash it. We would then spend the remainder of the day in a saloon somewhere, usually Novey's on Mulberry Street in Trenton, and always...always on the tab.

*   *   *

Pop did his drinking fastidiously. To him, it was an ancient and time-honored ritual. For years after Pop died, I could still form a mental picture of him sitting at the bar at Joe Novey's Mulberry Saloon, legs delicately crossed, fedora pushed back on his head, that badly set broken elbow from childhood sticking out at a crazy angle. Pop would raise a shot of Four Roses or some other brand of cheap whiskey neatly to his pursed lips and down the contents in one quick, efficient motion, grimacing slightly, then reaching for the short chaser of Piel's draft beer to wash down the whiskey. I usually had a ginger ale or something, pretending that we were knocking back the booze together. As far as lunch was concerned, Pop never "ate on an empty stomach," but I got hungry. When I would ask the old man for something to eat, Pop would have Novey drop a Stewart Infrared ham and cheese in the little oven behind the bar.

Pop was twenty years old when I was born. At that time, he was employed as a bus driver for Safeway Trailways, driving the New York-to-DC route. Pop was a master of his craft. He could park a big bus on a "gnat's backside," as he was fond of saying. Pop hated his Christian name of Wilbur and always insisted that his friends call him Bill. He always had a get-rich idea that never quite seemed to pan out. From time to time, he would leave his bus-driving work and embark on some new scheme, only to have his dream shattered by cold, hard reality. Pop always had partners for these ventures, and they were, like Pop, usually broke. Pop and a fellow Trailways driver named Mac McLane decided one afternoon while laying over in New York that they would agitate the drivers at Trailways to join a fledgling organization of their making titled the Coachman's Association. McLane was a real piece of work. He was a grizzled old-timer who, if he had a toothache, would simply take a pair of pliers, load up with an amount of Three Feathers whiskey that could bring an elephant to its knees, and drunkenly yank out the offending tooth. The end result of Pop's Coachman venture was that Trailways fired both Pop and McLane. The Coachman's Association, along with several of McLane's molars, died a quick and painful death.

Eventually Pop finally gave up his dream of unionizing bus drivers. His last effort had resulted in yet another visit to the ranks of the unemployed facilitated by two gentlemen who were the owners of a Trenton charter bus service, Starr Transit who had recently shown Pop the door at Starr for—surprise!—attempting to unionize the drivers.

As fate would have it, the Starr Transit garage was located on a side street barely one block from one of Pop's favorite (and there were many) hangouts, on East State Street, a neighborhood tavern that was owned by one of Pop's drinking cronies, one Darrell O. Barr—Pop always would refer to Darrell's establishment as "Mister Barr's bar." Darrell was a bartender from West Virginia who had migrated to Trenton and made enough money romancing rich women to open his own tavern. He and Pop had quickly become friends.

Darrell owned a vacant two-car garage next to the bar. During one afternoon at the tavern—an afternoon when many shots of Bushmills were reported to have been consumed—Pop convinced Darrell to enter into a partnership in a scheme to be named D&B Auto Glazers. The agreement was that Darrell would make the garage available and front the money for the buffer, pads, and liquid polish and Pop would do the physical labor of cleaning, applying the glaze, and buffing the surface of the automobile. As it was summertime and I was now sixteen and enjoying summer break, I pitched in with Pop to help out. Business cards and advertising fliers were printed. One of my friends and I drove to supermarkets and malls throughout the city, placing the advertising fliers under the windshield wipers of the parked cars. Official titles were bestowed, and the business was pronounced ready for the stream of customers bound to inundate the little garage. Pop would tell me of a time when they were sure to expand the business and just how that was to be accomplished. Plans were formulated, and we waited eagerly for the first customer.

The first customer of the tiny shop was a gentleman who owned a terribly oxidized 1953 Buick Roadmaster and who achieved the distinction of being the only customer that D&B Auto Glazers would ever service. After one month, Pop locked up the garage, withdrew to Darrell's saloon next door, and commiserated at length with the local barflies.

* * *

Ten years had passed since the D&B venture. I was half a world away, serving with the Navy, when word reached me of my father's death. Pop had died under mysterious circumstances. He had deteriorated further into alcoholism as the years had progressed. Finally, his wife had had enough and ordered him to leave their New England home. Pop had left, finding work as a bus driver for a company in New Brunswick. His alcoholism had been out of control. He had begun to gamble, and it was rumored that he was heavily into debt to the local New Brunswick bookies. He had reached bottom.

* * *

Pop had been absent from his work for several days. Telephone calls to his rented home went unanswered. One of his coworkers decided to check on him.

Pop's coworker found him in the garage, seated behind the steering wheel of his car. The car had been running until the gasoline in the tank had emptied. The garage door was closed, and there was a rubber hose attached to the exhaust pipe running into the car interior.

Pop had been dead for at least a day. An autopsy was never performed.

*   *   *

Lafayette Avenue

Although there was an abundance of kids on Lafayette Avenue, most of the families forbade their offspring to have anything to do with me. I had been classified a troublemaker early on, when I fed a box of Ex-Lax to the Rutkowski family's two boxers, which had resulted in the predictable response: the Rutkowski side yard resembled a rather squishy minefield of dog poop in less than one day. Mr. Rutkowski, a World War II veteran who brooked no nonsense, loved those dogs with a passion, and it was only the intervention of Mrs. Rutkowski that had prevented me from receiving the thrashing of my life.

And so because of the boxer episode and one or two other minor events, I was classified by the neighborhood families as a thoroughly bad influence. The kids of Lafayette Avenue were forbidden to associate with me. I had become a pariah in my very own neighborhood. There was to be no friendship with me by the kids on the block.

There were a few exceptions, the Schlegel family being one of the more notable. The Schlegels were of Pennsylvania Dutch origin, having moved to Trenton following World War II. The father, Lew, was a talented locomotive mechanic who was a complete alcoholic. Shortly after arriving in Trenton, the old man lost his job because of the booze and, as far as anyone could tell, never worked anywhere again. Lew Schlegel would occasionally leave his bedroom to come downstairs and sit in the parlor of the house and stare wistfully out of one of the parlor windows. There he'd sit and stare, very jaundiced and frail, saying very little. The old man was always very polite to me on the rare occasions that we would make eye contact. I felt sorry for this man who had long ago left his dignity and self-respect in the bottom of a whiskey bottle and was now slowly dying of chronic liver disease.

My empathy was not shared by the family. Old Lew had put them through too much heartache and disappointment for that. Mrs. Schlegel, Lew's wife, wouldn't hear of a divorce. She was a strong-willed churchgoing woman who held the family together on a low-paying state government clerical job and always found time to welcome me into her home as if I were part of the family. Often, she would haul out an ancient ice cream-making machine, crank handle and all, and make ice cream as a treat for her four children. She also had empty soda bottles that she would wash and use to store homemade birch beer to go with the ice cream. I suspected that she must have made that birch beer in the old wash tub—it always tasted a little soapy to me—but it was all that she could afford in the way of something special for the kids. Mrs. Schlegel had a backbone of pure steel. God had to have a special place reserved for her in Heaven.

The four children, Eleanor (Norie), Clara, Louie, and David, all helped around the house in different ways while the old man, his liver shot, lay upstairs in a bedroom, wasting away.

Norie was probably six years older than me and was a real looker. She had a good job somewhere and apparently spent most of her money on clothes, as she was always dressed much better than the rest of the family. Norie was a party girl. She was going to escape the poverty of her surroundings no matter what.

Clara was next oldest, about three years older.. Clara was the surrogate mother who took charge when Mrs. Schlegel was at work. She was constantly doing something around the house. She was also always listening to the latest pop hits on the radio and had a particular affinity for the Four Aces's "Heart of My Heart" and for just about anything sung by the Four Lads.

Louie was next in line, a year or so older than me and had a love for all things mechanical. He would sit in front of his house and talk of inventions that he was going to patent and how they would revolutionize society as they knew it. Louie was one of those incredibly energetic people whose mind was never in neutral. He could find immense pleasure in dissecting the inner workings of all types of household appliances, bicycles, electrical doodads—you name it. Try getting him to pitch in with a little yard work, and he would disappear in a hurry. Fix a lawn mower? That was fine. Operate one? Forget it. Eventually, Louie enrolled in a technical college in Pennsylvania, attending electronics classes in the evenings. He secured a day job at one of those mega auto dealerships in the area, turning back the speedometers on used cars.

David Schlegel was the youngest child. David was younger than Louie, about my age and was the quietest of the four Schlegel children. David wasn't particularly adventurous, nor was he the dreamer that Louie was. He was just an average good kid with a shy smile. David's clothes were always just a bit too big for him. They hung from his thin frame like the worn and faded hand-me-downs that they were. There was no money in the family budget for new clothes for David. It must have been terribly embarrassing for him to go to school and to church dressed like that. Everyone in the neighborhood felt sorry for David.

*   *   *

After a passage of more than sixty years I discovered in a musty attic photo album a picture of David that had been taken in the backyard of my house around 1951, when David had been ten. There he posed in that ancient, faded Kodak print, smiling shyly, wearing his brother's old clothes, looking exactly as I remembered him.

*   *   *

The Short Life of Francis Gravatt

Francis Gravatt—everyone called him Franny—was one of those kids who was destined to live a life embracing trouble. Franny was wild and uncontrollable. The rumor that made its way around my Broad Street Park neighborhood was that Franny's father would beat him unmercifully, often just on general principle. Those constant beatings had turned Franny into a hardened delinquent, unrepentant and oblivious to any punishment, whether the rumored whippings from his father or incarceration in the city juvenile shelter. Everyone in the neighborhood—including Franny—knew that he was well on his way to becoming a career criminal.

In spite of the admonition from my mother to stay clear of Francis Gravatt, I liked the promise of excitement and perhaps even danger when I was hanging out with Franny, and so I eagerly answered the door that September afternoon in 1950. After all, there was always an element of surprise on the days when we roamed the neighborhood, wasn't there?

"Wanna play some car chicken?"

"Dunno. What is it?"

My house fronted the south side of Broad Street, a four-lane street with the opposite travel lanes separated by a raised center grass median approximately three feet wide. As Franny explained to me the object of the game was to "run from the curb to the island and see how close we can come to the cars without getting hit. When we get there okay, then we run from the island back to the curb, but we have to get even closer to the car going back."

"Well.."

"Not scared, are you?"

"I'm not scared. Show me how you do it."

Franny then demonstrated to me how the game was to be played. He waited for southbound traffic to clear a bit and then successfully dashed across to the island, dangerously close to an oncoming car. The squeal of the car's tires while braking were followed by some very unusual language choices from the driver.

Franny just laughed. I couldn't see how Franny could possibly get any closer to an oncoming vehicle on the return dash without being hit and seriously injured.

I was right.

Franny stumbled slightly when he began the return trip from the center median to the curb. The car that he had chosen to challenge was a heavy four-door deSoto, which never slowed down.

WHUMP! The deSoto hit Franny and sent him flying down Broad Street for at least half a city block. Franny landed on the concrete highway in front of the Sunoco station in the next block. The station owner, Joe Roche, ran out to halt oncoming traffic, then gently lifted Franny's limp and motionless body and carried him to the curb before calling the ambulance service two blocks away.

The deSoto had broken nearly every bone in Franny's body. The force of Franny's brain slamming into his skull caused an inflammation so severe that a drain tube had to be inserted at the base of his skull to relieve the pressure. He remained hospitalized for several months before he was well enough to go home.

* * *

I had been granted two weeks' Christmas leave from the Navy before deploying to Vietnam the following month. My cousin Jack always knew where there was a party, and sure enough, he gave me a call to see if I wanted to go to one that evening. I agreed.

We arrived at the party host's apartment to find the festivities proceeding apace. I looked around the room to see if there were any familiar faces and spotted...Francis Gravatt!

It had been fifteen years since that fateful day when he had nearly been killed by the deSoto on Broad Street. Franny had bulked up considerably and told a tale of almost constant incarceration and trouble with the law. He was, he said, currently on parole from a burglary conviction and had determined that he wasn't going back to prison ever again.

I told Franny that I had spent the past eight years in the Navy, was planning to make a career of it, and, following the leave period, was deploying to Vietnam as part of an aviation tactical intelligence squadron aboard one of the newer aircraft carriers.

"We still have something in common after all this time," Franny said.

His remark aroused my curiosity. I jokingly remarked that I hoped that he wasn't about to suggest another round of car chicken.

He was not amused. Franny let the remark pass and said that he was the captain of a sixty-four-foot motor yacht, *Lanran*. The yacht was owned by Doctor James Dodge, a Broad Street general practitioner whose practice was three blocks west from my old Broad Street home. Franny had hired on as a deckhand and worked his way up to become the captain of Doctor Dodge's vessel.

Lanran was moored at the Trenton Marine Terminal, and Franny's job was to ensure that the motor yacht was kept seaworthy, as the good doctor often wished to take the yacht to Fort Lauderdale with a female not named Mrs. Dodge. As Doctor Dodge was no sailor, Franny was charged with getting *Lanran* safely to Fort Lauderdale and back. It was a terrific job, and Franny loved it.

After we chatted a bit more about our old neighborhood, Franny and one of the girls left the party.

* * *

It had been almost two years since I had returned to Trenton on leave, this time to visit my father's grave and quickly return to San Diego for counterinsurgency training. The flight to Philadelphia would take about four hours or so, and while I settled into my seat, I rummaged through the pouch on the back of the seat in the row ahead, looking for something to read. In the pouch was a copy of the *New York Times*.

I decided to read it anyway.

I skimmed through the first section and was going through the second when a story about a shipwreck off the coast of Cape Hatteras caught my eye.

The vessel's name: *Lanran*.

The newspaper article reported the details of a messy divorce between Trenton physician Doctor James Dodge and his wife. Mrs. Dodge had gotten wind of the Fort Lauderdale junkets of the good doctor and his companion and had filed for divorce. One of the marital assets was the *Lanran*. Attorneys for Mrs. Dodge had obtained a court order that required the *Lanran* to remain moored at the Trenton Marine Terminal while the divorce was being settled in court.

Dodge was having none of it. He had ordered Franny to make ready for sea. The *Lanran*, court order or no, was going to Fort Lauderdale.

Lanran got underway for Fort Lauderdale on August 9. Her passengers and crew had consisted of Dodge; his companion, twenty-eight-year-old Beverly Minotti; Minotti's three-year-old daughter, Kimberly; deckhand Christopher Brooks; and *Lanran's* captain, Francis Gravatt.

Two days later, after encountering heavy seas, *Lanran* had broken up and sunk with all aboard. Dodge, Minotti, Kimberly, and Franny were never found. Brooks had clung to a portion of the wheelhouse for three days before being picked up by a passing freighter.

My childhood friend Francis Gravatt was dead at twenty-eight. It has always seemed to me that God had, for some reason that we are not to understand, sentenced Franny to a lifetime of suffering and an early death.

I hope that Franny's reward has been kinder.

* * *

Necco Wafers

Mrs. Brown, confectioner to the kids of Schiller Avenue and beyond, earned her living one penny at a time. Her little confectionery had been fashioned from the front room of her Schiller Avenue home. Schiller Avenue was another of the same sort of working-class neighborhood streets that were part of my principal world, block after block of attached two-story, attic-topped homes fronted by an open sitting porch.

One block west and one block north of Schiller Avenue was the Carleton F. Willey Middle School, the local neighborhood school, which covered the fifth through seventh grades. I attended Willey for fifth and sixth grades in 1949 and 1950, until my mother decided that I needed more discipline and structure in my life. I was a year younger than my classmates, having skipped a grade a few years earlier. Every day for those two school years at the Carleton F. Willey Middle School, I would detour from my route to school (and sometimes on the way home, finances permitting) to stop at Mrs. Brown's candy store.

The store featured a glass display case that butted up against the front room wall, and within the confines of that case were sweet candies and other treats that that kids love to eat and upon which their family dentists become wealthy. The rest of the house was hidden from view by a curtain covering the entrance to the living quarters. The prospective customer would open the door, a little bell would ring, and Mrs. Brown, a large sixtyish woman whose gray hair desperately needed a comb, clad in an old house dress and well-worn apron, would enter wearily through the curtain to sell her confections. She had mostly penny candy and never lacked for customers from the middle school two blocks distant. Mary Janes, colored sugar drops stuck on paper, licorice sticks, tiny wax coke bottles containing colored syrup (the wax was chewed after the syrup was gone), candied mint faux cigarettes that came in pretend cigarette boxes, gumdrops, jelly beans, and my personal favorite, Necco wafers, were all on display and ready to be purchased and consumed.

It was candy heaven, and I seldom missed a day visiting Mrs. Brown's store.

The old woman made her living one penny at a time.

*   *   *

Cora

Francis Albert Sinatra's birthday is a day that, in my opinion, should be declared a national holiday. I thought it would be a nice tribute on that day to do a bit of YouTube research and post my three favorite Sinatra songs to my Facebook page. I had posted the first two, and while I was copying number three, I began to think about Cora.

*   *   *

It was the summer of 1967. The carrier task group to which I was attached had been operating in the Gulf of Tonkin, providing bombing interdiction over North Vietnam since early winter. The code name for our operating area was Yankee Station, which meant that we shared bombing duties with the Air Force over North Vietnam. After we had spent nearly sixty days at sea, working twelve hours a day, seven days a week, the relief carrier finally arrived and our big ship tied down her aircraft, stored the bombs securely in the ordnance magazines, wheeled one hundred and eighty degrees, and headed east across the South China Sea for the carrier pier at Subic Bay.

The transit to Subic would require three days. Olongapo City, with her endless array of bars, lovely young bar girls, and "rock" bands that always consisted of three guitars and a set of drums (the musicians never seemed to understand that when reaching the end of a song, they were all required to stop playing at the same time), here we come!

It was the second day of our Philippine transit when I received word that I was wanted in the Air Operations

Office to pick up a message that had arrived on the daily mail plane. Puzzled, I hustled up to Air Ops. Who would be sending me a message? Where had it originated? Was it bad news? These questions were buzzing inside my head when I entered the Air Ops shack. The duty officer handed me an envelope with only my name and rank written on the outside. No return address. No stamp. What in the name of heaven could this be about?

Enough speculation. I decided to open the damn thing on the spot. The note was from my old friend and former shipmate Gino. It simply read: "Take some leave. We're headed south to see Max." Gino and I had been stationed together several years past, and I assumed that the mysterious Max referred to in the note meant Max McNeil, who had also been stationed with us but had transferred out and hadn't been heard from since.

I submitted and was granted a leave request for the entire in-port period. Knowing Gino as I did, I knew that this leave period was bound to be a memorable one.

Day three dawned, and our carrier arrived at the Cubi Point carrier pier in Subic. Her crew was ready for some much-needed rest and recreation. I had packed my civilian clothes and was one of the first men to leave the ship when liberty was announced. Standing on the pier, waiting, was my friend Gino, a young Filipina woman, a Filipino man, and two portable ice chests. It was good to see Gino again after more than two years. He introduced me to the woman as his girlfriend, Minda, and the man as Rogelio. Rogelio, he said, was our chauffeur. The ice chests were filled with bottles of San Miguel beer and cheap Popov vodka.

Chauffeur? Why did we need a chauffeur, I inquired. Because, came the answer, we were headed southeast through the Zambales Mountains and around Manila Bay to Cavite City, where Max was living in high style in a walled villa. Oh, and by the way, Gino added, we'd be taking a live baby babuy with us.

Babuy? What on earth is a babuy? A baby pig, came the response. When we arrived at Max's place, we were going to butcher and roast the thing.

I reached into an ice chest and took a long pull from one of the vodka bottles that I found inside.

Rogelio was none too pleased that we'd be transporting livestock in the Navy Special Services Ford Fairlane that Gino had rented. Minda, speaking rapidly in Tagalog, assured him that she would fashion some diapers for the pig and that she would not only take care to see that it wouldn't soil the car interior but would also handle the delicate business of bribing the soldiers at the various checkpoints along the highway who were armed with automatic weapons and weren't afraid to use them if they perceived an affront to their delicate national honor. After much back-and-forth and the exchanging of a twenty-peso note, Rogelio reluctantly agreed to allow the pig to ride inside the car with us.

I took another long pull from the vodka bottle. I was going to need it if I was going to be part of this safari!

*   *   *

In the interest of brevity, I will shorten the narrative surrounding the long journey to Cavite City and report that the pig had a ripping good time riding in the front seat in Minda's lap, diapered to the nines with his snout sticking out the window like a dog. We managed to bribe our way through two checkpoints without getting shot by some very nervous soldiers. After several more pulls from the vodka bottle and a few San Miguels, both Gino and I were developing an affection for the damn pig riding happily in front and snorting at the passersby in the little barrios along the highway. We presented our case to Minda to spare the pig, but to no avail. The pig was to go to his reward the next day, skewered and slowly rotated over a fire pit.

Well, at least he enjoyed the car ride.

We arrived at Max's villa in the early evening. Max still looked exactly as I remembered him, a bit portly, bald, with a wide grin and an amiable affect. He ushered us inside the walls of the villa and introduced us to his "house girl." The house girl's job description evidently contained more than just taking care of the house—she was required to take care of Max also. Her welcome for our hardy band was less than enthusiastic. She viewed Minda as competition for Max and saw Gino and I as evil, vodka-swilling corrupters of Max's moral fiber.

I had news for the house girl: Max's moral fiber was thinner than dental floss.   The rest of the afternoon was spent unpacking and reminiscing about old times. The vodka bottles had long since emptied, and the San Miguel was running dangerously low. Max sent the girl out for more. On the way out the gate, she gave Gino the evil eye and disappeared into the dusky twilight.

*   *   *

After a late breakfast the next morning, Max announced that Minda and Evil Eye would be prepping and butchering the pig while he would show Gino and myself the town of Cavite City. Max had political connections with the local elected officials, as he was responsible for testing and evaluating Filipino citizens who wished to join the U.S. Navy through the seaplane base at Sangley Point. Sangley nestled up against Cavite City, and like navy towns everywhere, its main drag was populated with one bar after another. The first bar that we entered was owned by a former mayor of Cavite, a fellow named Peiping Arbanas. Arbanas owned several bars and restaurants and controlled the hiring and firing of virtually every bar girl in town. He and Max apparently had something going, something that I didn't want to know about. The four of us—Gino, Max, Peiping, and I—sat down over rum and cokes to pass the time. Every girl in the bar gravitated to our table.

"You like the girls?" Peiping, our host inquired. "No charge. Pick the one you want and no pay out to the bar. Just give the girl whatever you like." It was a bit early in the day, and I wanted to look around the rest of the town. I thanked Peiping for his generosity. Maybe later, I said.

After a few rums had been consumed, a young boy entered the bar, looking for Max. He hurried over to our table and announced that Evil Eye had paid him five pesos to follow us around and report back to her what we were doing in the bars. Max looked the kid in the eye, reached into his pocket, and handed him ten pesos. "What are we doing?" he asked.

"I don't see nothin'," came the reply. Smart kid.

As the day progressed into the afternoon, Max, Gino, and Peiping disappeared after huddling about something, and I decided to visit another watering hole to see what was happening. I left the bar, crossed the street, and sauntered into a ramshackle affair just up the main drag near the seaplane base. The jukebox in the place was playing loudly. I ordered a rum and coke and walked over to the jukebox to check out the playlist. It was a rather dated list, but it did contain a new Sinatra tune, "The Summer

Wind," that I hadn't heard. I put a few coins in the jukebox and selected the Sinatra tune.

The summer wind came blowing in, from across the sea...

I felt a nudge and turned to see a lovely young girl of seventeen or so. She had honey-blonde hair, bright blue eyes, skin the color of cocoa butter, and a pleasingly plumpish body that reminded me just a bit of Carroll Baker in the movie *Baby Doll*.

It lingered there and touched your hair and walked with me...

"Hi, sailor. I saw you sitting with Peiping at the other bar this morning." Her voice was a melody. "You're the one Max calls Bobby."

"I'd rather you called me Bob. What is your name?"

"Cora."

All summer long we sang a song, and then we strolled that golden sand...

We sat at a table, and I ordered a round of drinks. Cora asked for a Coke. We sipped and talked in that little run-down bar all afternoon. She was the daughter of a Filipina mother and American father who had left for the States before she was born and who, after promising to return for mother and daughter, was never heard from again. Cora didn't seem to mind. She was full of youthful optimism. She loved her world and wanted nothing more than to leave her family's nipa hut in the barrios to come to the bars and earn some pesos for herself and her family. Her effervescence and her mixed beauty captivated me.

Two sweethearts and the summer wind...

My heart was about to jump out of my chest.

"Cora, can you stay here in town with me at Max's house for a week or so?"

"Oh, sure. Max has a beautiful house. Can I take a shower when we get there? I always have to use a coffee can and a hose when I want to bathe."

"Of course you can. We'll even go and buy you some clothes so you have something more to wear. Tonight we're roasting a pig that we brought with us from Subic."

Cora giggled. "Okay, Bobby. Let's get going. I'm going to call you Bobby because I like that better."

"Bobby it is, baby doll. Let's get going."

* * *

We arrived back at Max's in the early evening. Cora was loaded down with shopping bags full of clothes that she had bought with the pesos I had given her. The babuy was roasting slowly in the fire pit. Every mongrel dog in the city was sitting outside the wall, hoping for Max to throw a scrap or two over the barrier, where they would fight like wolves for possession of the tasty morsel. Cora went immediately upstairs to find my room and the shower. Max, Gino, and I sat at the rattan bar, drinking rum and debating whether or not to listen to Armed Forces Radio. Soon, the pig was ready and we feasted on it, fire pit-baked potatoes, and some baked tropical roots or something that I cannot to this day identify. We had a marvelous evening laughing, drinking, and even being entertained by the women, who sang a few local songs in Tagalog. Evil Eye was no exception. She was as happy as I would ever see her, drinking San Miguel and flirting with Max. Max sat at the head of the table, eating and smiling benevolently, our gracious and generous friend and host. Our enjoyment obviously pleased him.

After dinner, we all pitched in to clear the table and straighten up the living and dining rooms while Evil Eye and Minda took care of the dishes. Cora volunteered somewhat halfheartedly to help, but Max said no, she was a guest of his friend and would not have to help. We spent the remainder of the evening laughing and talking and partaking of a native wine called *tubao*, made from coconut juice. It was late when Cora looked over at me and said in a small, shy voice that she was tired and wanted to go to bed. I agreed, and we said our goodnight to all and headed upstairs to my room.

The night was steamy and hot. There wasn't a breath of a breeze anywhere to be felt. I turned on the fan and directed it toward the double bed at the far wall. Cora came over to me and kissed me passionately. We stumbled across the room, undressed while still in an embrace, and fell into bed.

The world was new beneath a blue umbrella sky...

We made love passionately, hurriedly, quickly the first time, then tenderly and languidly for what seemed like forever, neither of us wanting it to end. After, Cora curled up in a little fetal-like ball and went to sleep, snoring softly. I remained awake, listening to her contented sound, before drifting off into a fitful sleep. I will never forget that evening.

The date was July 28, 1967.

The next morning over bloody Marys—Cora was having her usual Coke—we were planning to hire a jeepney to take us out to the barrios, where I was promised an authentic Filipino lunch. I was to meet her family and friends and just enjoy an afternoon in some little sari sari store somewhere, trying to keep up with the rapid Tagalog that all of the locals would be speaking. I guessed that my Tagalog was as rudimentary as was their English but Cora would be along to act as both my guide and translator. Later, we'd return to Max's and relax a bit before dinner.

We were just getting ready to leave when Max came rushing into the house with an official communication in hand. Our relief carrier, the *Forrestal*, had suffered a fire and explosion and was listing badly to port. At the time of the communication, the explosions had subsided but the fire remained out of control. All leave and liberty for our crew was canceled and all hands were to return to the ship immediately. If the ship had left Cubi Point, arrangements would be made for stragglers to fly back with the mail plane. Max had phoned Rogelio, who was staying at Sangley Point, and the car would be there within the half hour.

I was stunned, as was Gino. I looked over at my Cora and for one ever so brief moment, thought about disappearing into the barrio with her.

"Goodbye, Bobby. Go to your ship, and come back soon."

Cora came over to me, and we kissed for the very last time.

I lost you; I lost you to the summer wind.'

* * *

The Nu Pike

As amusement parks go, the Long Beach Nu Pike of the fifties was a heterogeneous affair, an amalgamation of seedy carny attractions, major amusement park rides, bars, a movie theater, and the Lido Ballroom, which boasted a live orchestra that played nightly. A sailor could take his girlfriend upstairs to the second-floor ballroom and trip the fancy along with the older group of couples who visited the Lido. The older group represented the last generation of couples that knew how to dance ballroom style. The orchestra would often mix in some of the newer dancing-style music with the older fox-trot charts, which not only gave the younger crowd a chance to get on the floor and show their newer style of dancing but also gave the older couples a chance to sit one out and catch their breath.

If dancing wasn't an option, there was the Strand Theater, which was nestled among the bars, souvenir shops, and shooting galleries along the promenade that offered mostly B movies and second-run films. Hardly anyone bought a ticket to actually watch the show. The couples who entered the Strand were there to take advantage of the darkness.

The main attraction of the Nu Pike was the Cyclone Racer, a huge roller coaster that featured dual parallel tracks, which dipped, swooped, and hurtled breathlessly downhill after being pulled to a dizzying height. Marvelous fun! When the cars from both tracks were filled to capacity, they would begin the ride simultaneously, with the occupants from each track cheering themselves on to win the dash back to the boarding platform.

Young sailors from the nearby naval station and shipyard would traverse the main promenade of the Nu Pike, trolling for young high school girls who were in turn looking to meet one of those peach-fuzzed young salts for an evening of fun along the Pike. Sailors who were twenty-one and older gravitated to the Hollywood Bar or the Carousel Bar along the promenade, looking to connect with older women who were not averse to inviting handsome young sailors home for the night, providing that their bar tabs were picked up by the lucky gobs.

Farther along the promenade, one passed the Laughing Lady Fun House, which was more of a house of horrors than a fun house. The balcony facing the promenade had a grotesque, mechanized mannequin, which was supposed to represent a happy, rotund lady. The mannequin was wired for sound that brought forth an evil, pseudo-jolly fat-lady-braying-type laugh, which seemed to warn the patrons that the fun house was not going to be as much fun as the sign promised.

Not much fun, indeed! The interior of the fun house was discovered one day to have an actual mummified corpse hanging from a noose tied to one of the rafters inside the attraction. For years, it had been assumed by everyone that the hanging man was just a dummy, but one day, a work crew inside the attraction took the dummy down to repair the beam from which it was hanging and, much to their—and everyone else's—surprise, found that it was an actual cadaver! After some research, the body was determined to be the mummified remains of one Elmer McCurdy, a minor Oklahoma outlaw who had been shot and killed at the age of thirty-one by a sheriff's posse in 1911. How Mr. McCurdy's remains found their way to the Laughing Lady is a story that may never be fully uncovered.

At the extreme eastern end of the promenade, very near the Cyclone Racer, was a carny-style sideshow. The tent that housed the show was fronted by a long raised wooden platform for the pitchman and his microphone to announce the attractions inside in his languid, mesmerizing baritone. Directly behind the platform were the large lurid hand-painted banners which depicted the attractions. The most unusual human abnormalities ever seen were on display for the audience to experience for the sum of only one quarter of a dollar. The show was in fact only marginally different from those seen in the traveling carnivals of earlier times when the "hayseeds" at the county fairs were deemed gullible enough to pony up and venture inside.

Once a valued addition to any traveling carnival or tent circus, by the 1950s, the sideshow was a vanishing phenomenon on the American scene, partly because of the trend toward demystifying science and medicine, and partly because of its own seedy charade. The two-headed boy advertised on the large canvas poster outside was nothing more than a fetal miscarriage bathed in formaldehyde in an old pickle jar. The monkey girl? A microcephalic child of more than sixty years, the product of some past coupling of two people too directly related, which produced an exploited child whom no one wanted.

The owner of the Nu Pike sideshow was Tony Marino, a Mexican in his early sixties who had learned his profession as a member of any number of the traveling carnivals both in Mexico and stateside. Tony was the backbone of the show. He was the fire-eating act, the sword-swallowing act, the knife thrower, the illusionist who would saw in half Sandy, the overweight, world-weary middle-aged woman clad in net stockings and tights. Tony could perform any of the acts except for Bobby the Human Pincushion and the hypnotist demonstration performed by the show pitchman, Claude. Bobby was an affable, slightly built young gay man from somewhere in L.A. with obvious masochistic tendencies. He was covered with tattoos, and his act consisted of skewering himself with very long, very large, very sharp needles. Many of the patrons who paid their quarter were revolted by Bobby's act, yet they could not look away. Bobby and his needles were morbidly fascinating to them.

Claude the hypnotist was a long-faced, baritone-voiced man who doubled as the pitchman and show hypnotist. He had a steady, calming voice that captured just about all who came within earshot. Claude was the perfect front man for the attraction. He charmed the passersby outside and brought them in, and then Tony took over, beginning with his fire-eating act. When it came time for Claude to do his hypnotist routine, there was always someone—usually a young woman—more than willing to go onstage and be mesmerized by his soothing baritone, long black cape, and oscillating pocket watch.

Over time and after many twenty-five-cent visits to that run-down old show, I got to know Tony and his crew and have often thought about just exactly what was so fascinating to me about Tony Marino and his entourage those many years past. Part of it was listening to the stories that Tony would relate to his friends about his years on those dusty back roads as part of those long-ago traveling carnivals working in those past gypsy-like carny days, but after the passage of more than a half century, I also think it was the fact that I was witnessing a piece of Americana that had begun in an earlier century and was rapidly vanishing from the American landscape. Tony and his associates were an anachronism, relics of a robust and individualistic time since gone by.

* * *

Billy Pieslak

One common bond that formed our brief friendship—perhaps the only bond—was that both Billy Pieslak and I came from fatherless homes. I could never remember the time when my mother, father and I had lived together as a family unit in the same home. I had seen the old photographs, those Kodak black-and-white snapshots that had the NevrFade trademark with the early 1940s dates stamped on the back that were from the time when I was still a toddler, but those photos were completely foreign to me, as I had been very young when my mother and father had dissolved the marriage and gone their separate ways. The only immediate family unit that I knew consisted of my mother, my grandmother, my grandmother's boarder, Hoppy and me. We lived in the big house on Broad Street next to the truck-repair garage.

Billy Pieslak's home situation was completely, tragically different from mine. Billy's father, Joe, a twice-wounded combat veteran of World War II, had fought his way through North Africa, Sicily, and the Italian peninsula and managed to survive the carnage to return to his family in Trenton. Freida, Billy's mother, always seemed to be on the verge of a nervous breakdown. Her anxiety, which had taken hold during the war while worrying constantly over the prospect of losing her husband to a well-aimed Nazi bullet during the four years of his absence, had never really subsided. It was as if she'd had some premonition of impending doom that no one else could envision. Everyone in the neighborhood said that Freida Pieslak was just a worrier, a person who would not and could not allow herself to be content. Freida always affected an air of approaching catastrophe.

As fate would have it, Freida Pieslak's premonition turned out to be horribly correct. Sergeant Joe Pieslak, recently discharged honorably from the United States Army and who had been awarded the Bronze Star and two Purple Hearts, was killed while crossing Broad Street on his way to the barbershop to get a haircut, run down by a Trenton Transit charter bus that was ferrying new recruits to the Army basic training center at nearby Fort Dix. Joe had been home for less than two months. Compounding the irony surrounding the cause of Joe Pieslak's death was the fact that the driver of the bus was a Mr. Tifton, whose extended family owned the bake shop just three doors away from Billy Pieslak's house. Freida, a frequent customer of the Tifton family bakery until Joe's untimely death, never set foot in the bake shop again.

By the time Billy and I had become friends, it had been more than six years since Joe Pieslak's death, and Billy seemed to have taken the whole affair more or less in stride. Billy had really only known his dad for the two months before Joe had been killed. His dad had gone off to war when Billy was an infant, and he'd had no memory of his father at all. It was if a strange man had returned to live in the house with Billy and his mother for those two months prior to the accident.

Billy's mother never recovered from Joe's death. She had received a settlement from the bus company that allowed her to remain at home and micromanage Billy's every waking moment. The safety of Billy Pieslak consumed nearly her entire day. She hated for him to leave the house. If he had to cross Broad Street, she would stand on the front sitting porch and worriedly scan both directions of the street for oncoming traffic, shouting, "Run, Billy!" or "Now, Billy!" whenever she felt that traffic was sparse enough for him to safely get across. Her physical appearance deteriorated. She rarely dressed to go out of the house, instead donning a housecoat and slippers for her daily wear. She remained housebound, loath to leave the security of her home. Her hair was unkempt, and she eschewed makeup of any kind. Every Wednesday, she would give Billy cash and a list of groceries to purchase at the nearby A&P supermarket rather than go herself.

Billy was of course terribly embarrassed by his mother and would tell his friends that she had "gone nuts" since his father's death. His mother would always have some reason why Billy should stay home. On the rare times when he convinced her to let him leave, she would demand a complete itinerary: Who were the friends he was going to see? Where would they be going? What would they be doing when they got there? When would he return home? Would he be near a telephone in case his mother needed him? When he got there, would he call her with the telephone number? Billy would nod his head, dutifully answer her questions, promise to telephone her with a number where he could be reached, and then proceed to ignore her demands completely, preferring instead to suffer his mother's anguish and her attempts to educate him into guilt upon his return. Her theatrics went in one ear and out the other. He had heard them too often.

Billy Pieslak was quite strong, well-muscled and fit far beyond others his age. His mother had purchased a set of weights that he kept in the cellar that he religiously used every day. In addition to working out, he loved to box and had fashioned a small boxing ring, which consisted of nothing more than a padded 12' x 12' mat laid out on a portion of the cellar floor. He would routinely invite his friends down to his makeshift gym, hand them boxing gloves, and invite them to spar with him. At one time or another, all of his friends had stepped into that ring with him, but only briefly; after a few licks from Billy's right hand, his adversary of the moment would holler uncle and promptly withdraw. Billy had many sparring partners while growing up, but I cannot recall anyone who volunteered to step in that ring with him more than once.

Billy was just a bit slow-witted, what people referred to as "strong as an ox and twice as dumb." When he spoke, his speech impediment made him difficult to understand. He didn't do very well with his school studies and had been left back one year, which made him older than his classmates and the butt of many cruel jokes—none of which were spoken when he was within earshot. There were too many testimonials regarding that killer right-hand punch that he had honed to perfection. He allowed some ribbing from his friends, as they were his ticket out of the house and away from his mother, but everyone knew that the ribbing had definite boundaries. When he stopped smiling, it was definitely time to back off!

When he was seventeen, Billy got a job as a soda jerk at Friedman and Frompkin's drugstore on the corner of Broad Street and Harrison Avenue, which was located one block from his house. Mrs. Friedman outfitted him with one of those paper soda-jerk hats and somewhere managed to find a short-waisted white jacket that barely contained Billy's bulging muscles. He looked like a bit actor from one of those forties teen movies. His friends knew that he tended to panic when his brain received too much information for him to process, and so two or three of them would descend on the soda fountain when he was working and order something different from the fountain at once, which would throw poor Billy into a state of panic. He would always get those orders mixed up and have to start again from the beginning.

It was at about that time – I, too had just turned seventeen- that I managed to convince my mother to sign a waiver that would allow me to join the Navy. My mother was more than happy to do so. "Maybe you'll get your bearings and learn a trade while you're there," she said. Papers were signed, physicals were taken, oaths of allegiance were sworn, and I departed for the Great Lakes Naval Training Center just three weeks prior to Christmas of 1957.

*   *   *

Seven years had lapsed since I had last seen Billy Pieslak. I was now a career Navy man of twenty-four and had returned home on leave for a Christmas visit with my family. While home, I had met a lovely young woman at a neighborhood tavern and we had been keeping steady company for the duration of my leave period. One afternoon I decided to shop downtown for a present for the young woman. My first stop was Arnold Constable's, the upscale department store located on State Street in the heart of the city. As I was walking toward the jewelry counter, I saw a familiar face. It was Billy Pieslak, dressed in a coat and tie—the coat could barely contain those bulging muscles—who had been working as a security officer at the store for the past few years.

Billy said that what he really wanted in life was to join the Army and try out for the Green Berets but that if he did, his mother said that she would kill herself.

*   *   *

Devil's Bend

Overlook Avenue was the shabbiest street in the neighborhood. Only one block in length, the street consisted of attached row houses, many of which were in disrepair. The breadwinners of these run-down homes were mainly laborers who held jobs as hod carriers and other menial positions that barely paid a living wage. Overlook Avenue was a down-at-the heels street in a lower-class blue-collar neighborhood. During the postwar recession, the neighbors who lived on the nearby streets who found themselves struggling to keep their heads above water could comfort one another by saying, "Well, at least we don't have to live on Overlook."

Several of my classmates in fifth and sixth grade at Willey School came from Overlook Avenue. The girls were for the most part very good students. They were quiet, were attentive in class, and always turned in their homework assignments on time. The Overlook boys, in contrast, were rowdy, thuggish, and completely indifferent when it came to schoolwork. One or two of them went so far as to attempt to extort classmates for their lunch money every day. The Overlook boys were a mean-spirited lot who were said to be carbon copies of their drunken, brutish fathers.

The street was aptly named, as it fronted a rather overgrown and unkempt wooded area that my friends and I knew only as The Lake. An angular sloping and rutted drop of some two hundred feet leading to a spring-fed lake of some twenty-plus acres that had fallen into disrepair and disuse. Dirt pathways, eroded trails along the slopes, underbrush, hanging vines, and tall grass made for great pretend jungle war games that we would play during the warmer months of the year. The first winter snowfall brought the cessation of the war games and the arrival of neighborhood kids with their Flexible Flyer sleds to Devil's Bend, a somewhat hazardous, wildly eroded sloping and serpentine pathway that began at the foot of Overlook Avenue and continued its reckless journey to the lakefront at the bottom. One at a time, a sledder would get a running start, belly flop on top of his sled, and careen wildly toward the lakefront at the bottom of the trail. It was an exhilarating ride, twisting, turning, and banking along the Devil's Bend trail, providing that the sledder made it all the way to the bottom, which was usually not the case. Often, the rider would slide wildly off the eroded trail and separate from the sled, tumbling head over heels toward the lakefront. The kid with the worst wipeout would have the bragging rights right up until the next sledder began his descent. It was, as my friend Del often said, "one hell of a ride."

The overgrown and weed-infested lake was once the garden spot of Central New Jersey. It was said that during the nineteenth century, tourists from as far away as Hightstown and Burlington made the journey to visit Boiling Spring Lake. In those twilight days of the previous century, it was a prime area for picnicking. Tables and benches were placed along verdant lawns underneath elm trees for the families who brought lunch with them for an outing and an alfresco dining experience. Couples strolled the flower-and-shrubbery-lined pathways that led to a suspension bridge that crossed over Boiling Spring Lake where ice-cold springwater rose to the lake surface. Every Saturday afternoon, an orchestra performed in the bandshell for the picnickers' listening pleasure. Many a happy couple became betrothed in the beautiful gardens of the Boiling Spring.

The main entrance to the Boiling Spring Lake was located at the foot of Harrison Avenue, where a three-story gabled hotel stood for those who wished to remain overnight. Horse-drawn trolleys of the Trenton Traction Company would stop in front of the hotel, and the park visitors would walk some fifty yards inland to a platformed cascade of ornate stone steps that descended to the park below.

*   *   *

The dawning of the twentieth century brought change to Boiling Spring Lake. In 1907, a group of investors formed a company known as the White City Company to develop the Boiling Spring Lake area into an amusement park. A roller coaster was constructed, as were a dance hall, merry-go-round and other attractions. The finished buildings and rides were all painted white. The price of admission to the White City Amusement Park was the princely sum of one thin dime. At the park's heyday, as many as twenty thousand visitors per week would board the Trenton Traction Company trolley for the ride to the park, but by the 1920s, the park was abandoned as the public's obsession for the automobile grew. There was simply no place to park the visitors' cars. Over the years, lumber salvagers tore down the rides and buildings, and the park, once thought of as the main leisure attraction of Central New Jersey, became overgrown with weeds and filled with debris.

The hotel closed its doors and fell into disrepair. The widow of the owner and her mentally disabled son, whom the neighborhood kids cruelly called Crazy Jack, were the only two who remained in the large structure. The older residents of the neighborhood said that the old woman who remained in the now closed and run down hotel with her son practiced some kind of sorcery in the upstairs part of the hotel. Grandmothers cautioned against getting too close to Crazy Jack, who rode his bicycle throughout the Broad Street Park neighborhood, a Lucky Strike cigarette dangling from his mouth. It was rumored that if a child came too close to Jack, he would snatch the child up with one powerful hand and ride off to deliver the unfortunate moppet to the old woman in the hotel. Whenever Jack rode by on his bicycle, mothers would quickly grab their infant children and take them inside.

As for Boiling Spring Lake, only the stone staircase was left, an ornate remnant of the garden spot of a time that had long since passed.

We didn't care. We had Devil's Bend.

* * *

III.

Stories Adapted from Counting Coup: The Odyssey of Captain Tom Adams

Mal de Mer

Excerpts from the journal of Captain Thomas A. Adams, recently mustered out of the Union Army following the cessation of hostilities of the War of Southern Aggression, having fought valiantly and with much distinction.

June 21, 1865. Lancaster, Pennsylvania

In all candor I must say that, having survived the carnage of Chancellorsville and Gettysburg during the recent War of Southern Rebellion as a cavalry captain of the 8th Pennsylvania Brigade and having witnessed many acts of both bravery and suffering during these bloody contests, the prospect of returning home to farm the lands of my dear father and mother holds little sway over me. I have informed my dear parents of my desire to proceed westward to seek new adventures. This has caused my dear mother much heartbreak and sadness. My father refuses to speak of this decision and indeed has informed me that my share of his lands will be given to my younger brother Jacob. This is as it should be, for Jacob is a man born to till the soil and raise livestock. I on the other hand have no desire to embrace a life wedded to the soil. I have received a substantial mustering-out pay from the army and, having researched the many methods available for trans-continental travel, have decided on a sea passage around the southern tip of South America which will eventually deliver me to the Golden Gate, a land of both opportunity and adventure! I shall book passage on the SS Orient Queen bound for Colon, Callao, and the Golden Gate.

July 1st. At sea

We have cleared the New York harbor and have set a southerly course for the Drake Passage. New and exciting adventures await me. I am barely able to contain my high spirits.

Excelsior!

July 3rd. At sea aboard the *SS Orient Queen*

Our ship is a magnificent vessel, a three-masted steam-powered side-wheeler of four thousand tonnes with a capacity for one thousand passengers—although there are considerably fewer than that number for this voyage—with cargo holds for freight and mail as well. She rides extremely well on the open sea and will no doubt withstand the formidable winds and high seas that we will encounter as we transit the Drake Passage at the very tip of the Southern Hemisphere, the frigid and inhospitable bottom of our earth. Our ship's purser goes by the name of Dewksberry, a man of some fifty-plus years who claims to have made the perilous journey many times. Mr. Dewksberry, when primed with a dram or two of brandy from the passenger salon, has the annoying habit of mesmerizing the distaff passengers with tales of peril surrounding our impending transit of the Drake Passage. He paints a grim picture indeed, one of floating icebergs and fifty-foot waves, of ships being rendered helpless and driven to destruction on the rocky shoreline of Patagonia and men being swept over the side into the icy waters of the Passage. His remarks have caused much distress among the embarked passengers, and some have even threatened to debark upon reaching Colon, our first port of call, to book passage on the next vessel bound for New York. Fortunately, cooler heads have prevailed, mine being one of them, that have pointed out to these distressed travelers that Dewksberry was well in his cups when recounting his revelations and was more than likely endeavoring to elevate his own self-importance. I have no use for this besotted alarmist. My fellow passengers would be well advised to keep the man's nose far removed from the brandy keg.

Speaking for myself I am quite keen to observe this notorious body of water that is so far removed from my upbringing on the family farm in Pennsylvania.

July 10th. Colon, Panama

We have stopped at the very edge of the jungle! The narrow dirt paths that are the only substitute for roads are lined with row after row of warehouses and ramshackle living quarters that house the native stevedores who load and unload the merchant ships that visit the port. As far as I can see, there is no other function here other than to service the ships that call with their various cargoes. Some of my fellow passengers have debarked here, as they represent the various business interests located in this steaming, hot, mosquito-infested dismal intrusion into the Colombian Protectorate. A few engineers and surveyors have also departed, as they have arrived to begin studying the terrain for a fellow by the name of de Lesseps who, it is rumored, wishes to construct a canal through the Isthmus to the Pacific Ocean, which would drastically reduce the transit time between oceans. They have their work cut out for them, if I may be forgiven a pun.

A steward has rigged our beds with mosquito netting, and we have been advised to sleep under said netting each night while we remain in port. We have also been advised to drink only wine that has been laced with a bitter powder known as quinine, as there is an extremely high incidence of malaria, yellow fever, dysentery and other tropical maladies that are endemic to this Godforsaken part of the world.

July 13th. On the high seas

We have shown our stern to that cursed corner of earth that is Panama and are once again underway for our next port of call, which is Callao, Peru, by way of the Drake Passage at Cape Horn. Our ship's captain is a large, red-faced fellow by the name of Stewart who sports a formidable set of muttonchops and gives every indication that his entire life has been spent as a seafaring man. Captain Stewart seems to me to be a seasoned mariner who has seen all that King Neptune has to offer. He has informed us that the Southern Hemisphere winter sea conditions will be encountered and that due to fuel considerations, we will be making only ten knots of speed and possibly less when we enter the Drake Passage. The Captain has also informed us that the loquacious Mr. Dewksberry will not be joining us for the remainder of the voyage, as he has been unceremoniously sacked when an audit of his receivables ledger revealed numerous inconsistencies. Our new purser is a fellow of Philippine extraction by the name of Romeo Arbanas. Mr. Arbanas is a hard-working fellow who abstains from alcohol and prefers to do his duty rather than socialize with the passengers. I like him. My landlubber's calculations suggest that we will arrive at the Drake Passage in roughly eleven days. I am experiencing both excitement and apprehension mounting within me!

July 23rd. Off the Islas de los Estados

The barometer in the passenger lounge is plunging downward at an alarming rate. Captain Stewart, in his usual laconic fashion, has opined that it would appear that the Orient Queen is "In for a blow." We are currently steaming along a south-southwesterly track and at day-break will come about to a more westerly course to enter the Passage, leaving the South Atlantic behind in our frothy wake. Our first mate has informed us that Orient Queen is currently experiencing fifteen-degree rolls and the forecast is exceedingly gloomy. He has advised the passengers to don their life vests as a precaution. A great many of the passengers, including myself, are coping with varying degrees of Mal-de-mer, yet in spite of this I am able to keep this journal current although I cannot say for how much longer.

July 25th. Drake Passage transit

Cartographers may well refer to this dark and fore-boding body of water as the Drake Passage, however as far as I am concerned it is the portal into Hell. There can be no doubt that a watery grave will be the fate of the Orient Queen and those aboard her. We have begun this transit at the height of a winter storm. Captain Stewart has ordered all passengers to remain clear of all weather decks and to remain in their respective cabins. I cannot possibly imagine why anyone would care to venture out on deck in this hellish maelstrom. The ship is taking forty-degree rolls and the captain has steered the bow of the ship directly into the storm, as this will greatly reduce the chance of her capsizing when trapped in the trough created by the monstrous sea swells that we now attack head on. Whenever we encounter one of the forty-foot monsters, the ship rises up, her bow completely out of water, and remains suspended in midair for what seems to be an eternity, shuddering mightily and then crashing down into the roiling seas with a force that seems certain to have dislodged the very rivets that keep her together, yet she plows ahead, barely making headway, her engines racing at full power merely to keep our bow on aspect into the storm.

All outside and inside hatches, doors and portholes have been secured, as have the cargo hold covers. There remains a constant concern that the cargo stored in the ship's hold could come unsecured and shift, which surely would cause us to capsize.

Mr. Arbanas has assured me that these are merely precautionary measures but I have the rather disconcerting idea that someone in the pilot house, perhaps Captain Stewart himself, is of the opinion that we may well succumb to the turbulence outside.

I have never felt so helpless.

July 26th.

I am now certain that I am near death. My flesh has taken a morbidly green hue and I am violently nauseated. If this damned vessel is to capsize, let it be sooner rather than later. A quick death is preferable to this prolonged agony. I have not eaten a bite in two days and yet I still retch violently whenever the ship rolls with one of the monstrous waves. Arbanas has provided each passenger with a supply of crackers, as the galleys have been secured for the remainder of the storm. The very sight of them exacerbates my condition.

Oh sweet death, where, o where, is thy sting!

July 28th. Cape Horn

It would appear that I am not destined to go to my reward after all! My flesh is gradually returning chameleon-like to its normal hue and I have even entertained the thought of partaking of one of Mr. Arbanas' crackers that were given the passengers to sustain them as we fought the vicious storm that God had visited upon us. Moreover, Arbanas has informed me that according to the captain's dead reckon plot, we have finally embraced the waters of the Pacific and that the worst has passed. Can it be that I will soon be able to embrace my normal dietary habits?

Earlier this afternoon I unfastened the toggles that secured my cabin porthole, as I wished to see firsthand the state of the seas that had been tossing us about like a cork for the past several days. There does look to be signs of the storm's abatement, as the skies which had been so ominously black seem to have lightened a bit and the ship's propulsion engines sound considerably less labored than they had earlier. We seem to be moving forward at a somewhat faster pace, and Arbanas says that we have been able to resume our westerly track. The word has been passed that we may remove our life jackets and that the dining facilities will shortly be resuming their normal schedule.

Apparently our captain sees smooth sailing ahead. Praise God!

July 29th. Off Diego Ramirez Island

The sun has reappeared, the seas have subsided and I have experienced the pleasure of a stroll on deck for the first time in nearly a week. The air is clean and crisp, the sky has an exceptionally bright blue hue and I am experiencing a euphoric sense of the sheer joy of life itself! We are headed on a northerly course for our next port of call—Callao, Peru—where we will remain for several days to discharge and receive both passengers and cargo. A feeling of camaraderie has developed among our passengers from having shared and survived the danger of the winter storm while transiting the Passage. It would come as no surprise to me that many of my fellow travelers had resigned themselves to meet their maker—as had I—while enduring the "blow," as our laconic captain has described that descent into Hell.

Arbanas has informed us that we expect to enter Callao on the August 8th tide. I can hardly contain my excitement! My very first trip abroad, and I will be visiting an exotic port in a strange continent.

August 9th. Callao, Peru

It has been more than one month since I have set foot on dry land, and while the thought of solid ground beneath my feet is a comforting one, I have the rather odd sensation that the very ground beneath me is swaying gently to and fro as if I were still at sea. I am certain that my normal equilibrium will soon return, and yet the sense of Terra firma swaying beneath my boots is a bit confusing. Mr. Arbanas has informed me that this anomaly will pass quickly, but his assurances are of little comfort to a land-lubber such as myself. I have promised myself that upon reaching San Francisco I shall never go to sea upon the open oceans again.

The afternoon while bright and sunny is decidedly cool and breezy. I have been advised to bring a coat ashore, and as I possess only my old army tunic at the present, it will have to suffice until I reach my destination. While I was at first somewhat bewildered by the coolness of the climate I recalled our captain's remark that the seasons are reversed in the southern hemisphere: while Lancaster, Pennsylvania is experiencing what I would imagine to be very hot summer days it is the winter season here.

Our stay in Callao has been truncated, as our ship needs to reach San Francisco in order to effect repairs sustained during our battle with the elements of the Drake Passage. The captain has decided to get underway on the August 10th tide. There is feverish activity from both the native stevedores and the ship's crew to load Orient Queen and make her ready for sea.

August 16th. At sea

What a glorious day to be alive! Today has been another of those absolutely perfect days to be at sea. Indeed, the weather has made for excellent sailing ever since our Callao departure. Orient Queen glides effortlessly through a calm sea of deep blue, her engines humming quietly. Her great side wheels leave a frothy wake of white phosphorescence behind us, a temporary signature attesting to the fact that we have passed by and which will be reclaimed by the very water that we have so rudely disturbed. The sky is a beautiful azure blue punctuated by tufts of fluffy white cumulus clouds. The forward motion of our vessel provides a gentle and refreshing breeze across our decks. After four years of the senseless carnage of war and a harrowing journey through the Drake Passage I am once again at peace with mankind and in awe of the wondrous creations of our Lord.

Ten days until our arrival at the port of San Francisco. Who can say what adventures await me in the pearl of the Golden Gate as I seek my fate?

*   *   *

Captain Adams Meets the Emperor

It was the morning of August 29, and the Union Street Wharf in San Francisco was its usual turbulent and noisy locus of commercial activity. Stevedores loaded and unloaded pier-side cargo from the docked vessels while ships officers shouted orders to the ordinary seamen engaged in securing their respective ships' decks and rigging for sea. Muscular workhorses pulled drays loaded with freight from the wharf for delivery to merchants in the city and beyond. The air was heavy with the smell of creosote and canvas mingling with the faint odor of salt air and decomposing fish parts carelessly thrown into the water, where other fish would dispose of the unwanted heads and entrails.

Captain Tom Adams, recently mustered out from the 8th Pennsylvania Cavalry, worldly possessions packed in his valise, Army-issue Spencer .52-caliber repeating rifle and Remington Army .44-caliber revolver holstered, sheathed, and secured to the side of the valise, stood by the brow of the *Orient Queen* waiting for a carriage or wagon for hire that would transport him into town. He would have to secure temporary lodging prior to setting out for the western interior. A good horse and saddle and warm clothing for the approaching winter months had to be purchased as well, and the expense of room and board while he was in San Francisco would tax his already dwindling stake. No question about it, he would have to find work in order to begin his quest.

First things first: Find transportation into town, secure temporary lodging in a local hotel or boarding-house, and prepare for the trek inland.

Adams had been pier side for thirty minutes or more before he was offered a ride in a two-team wagon loaded with freight that was heading into San Francisco proper. Upon questioning, the driver recommended a boarding-house in downtown San Francisco on Commercial Street, the Eureka Boarding House for Gentlemen.

* * *

August 30th. San Francisco

The driver of the Wells Fargo cartage wagon, a most agreeable fellow, has taken me directly to the Eureka and I have secured lodging for the quite reasonable sum of five dollars per week. The proprietress is a Mrs. Chambers, a widow of some fifty-odd years. She has shown me my room on the second floor which is rather sparsely furnished but clean and comfortable-looking and includes breakfast each morning promptly at seven. There is a bath with running water at the end of the hall that will allow me to perform my morning ablutions. Today and tomorrow will be devoted to settling in and orienting myself as to the city streets. Following this I shall begin searching for a position of employment, possibly as an armed guard, as I have had extensive experience with firearms for the preceding four years.

August 31st. San Francisco, 0630 hours

This morning as I was preparing to use the hall bath I became acquainted with the gentleman who occupies the room across from me. Exiting the bath, he introduced himself to me with a booming voice and sweeping bow as Norton I, Emperor of these United States and Protector of Mexico! I must say that he hardly looked the part to me clad only in his undershirt and braced trousers. While the man seems a bit unbalanced, he does not appear to be a danger. I returned his bow as grandly as I could muster and returned his greeting with an "honored to make your acquaintance, excellency." The Emperor gave me a rather suspicious look and continued on to his quarters. I expect we shall meet again at the breakfast table.

August 31st. San Francisco, 0800 hours

Breakfast this morning was hearty fare indeed. Hot coffee, eggs, fried bread and—scrapple! Evidently Mrs. Chambers must have Pennsylvania roots, as I have not tasted this treat in quite some time. I must remember to ask her about this eastern delicacy.

His Excellency the Emperor graced us with his presence at table this morning clad in his full regalia consisting of baggy gray trousers covering well-worn boots, a rather tatty Union general officer's coat replete with yellowed epaulets, and an officer's saber attached to the military belt surrounding his waist. Atop his rather shaggy and unkempt head was a beaver-pelt top hat which looked to be in some disrepair. In the hatband were placed large and colorful feathers which appear to have been plucked from a peacock. His ensemble was garnished by the presence of a rather handsome and ornate walking cane. As he approached the table, the several other men who were seated rose deferentially and greeted the man. I was so taken aback by this display that I remained seated, fascinated by the spectacle before me and unable to utter so much as a syllable.

*   *   *

His Excellency, Norton I, Emperor of the United States of America and Protector of Mexico, had arrived for his morning meal with a sheaf of papers in his hand.

"Good morning, gentlemen, Mrs. Chambers. Please take your seats and resume your repast. Mrs. Chambers, we will have a full breakfast this morning, if you please, as we have much to accomplish today. We have an imperial proclamation to deliver to Mr. Clemens at the *Herald* and to our loyal subjects, and we are to be fitted for a new field uniform at Mr. Costa's custom tailor shop. Following the sartorial measurements, we shall exercise Lazarus and Bummer for their morning constitutional and survey the streets for cleanliness."

Lazarus and Bummer? Adams wondered who they might be.

The emperor sat down to breakfast, and everyone resumed their meal. Mrs. Chambers scurried into the kitchen to prepare the emperor's breakfast. Apparently, the house residents humored this man, who was obviously a bit off center line. They actually seemed to enjoy his presence, and Adams could sense that they considered it great sport to give the old man exaggerated deference.

Norton began to circulate copies of his latest proclamation to the guests at the table. When he reached Adams, he paused a moment, eyeing Adams's Army tunic, and handed him a copy of the edict.

"Sir, we will have a word with you following breakfast."

Adams, still somewhat dumbfounded, nodded in agreement. He took the paper and began to read.

A Proclamation

Being desirous of allaying the dissensions of party strife now existing within our realm, we do hereby dissolve and abolish the Democratic and Republican parties, and also do hereby decree the disenfranchisement and imprisonment for not more than ten, nor

less than five, years of all persons leading to any viola-tion of this, our imperial decree.

Having distributed the proclamation to the breakfast guests, the emperor turned to Adams and addressed him.

"We notice that you are wearing the tunic of an offi-cer of our army, and we are in need of a military escort this day as we discharge our royal duties to the citizenry of San Francisco. You shall have this important office and accom-pany us this day as our military liaison."

Adams demurred.

"Sir, with all respect due your office, I am no longer an officer in the army. I was mustered out last spring after the surrender at Appomattox. I have business to attend today in order to prepare for a journey inland."

The emperor gave Adams a withering stare while demolishing a slice of Mrs. Chambers's scrapple.

"No matter. We hereby appoint you as colonel. We desire that you accompany us today. Lazarus and Bummer will join us as we attend to the affairs of the realm."

The emperor placed emphasis on his edict with a loud belch, a testimonial to Mrs. Chambers's scrapple.

Lazarus and Bummer again. What in the world was the man talking about? Adams glanced at the other residents at the table. They were obviously amused at his discomfort. They were making every effort not to laugh out loud.

Everyone at the table was amused except for one man, who was seated at the table head. He was looking directly at Adams with a slight frown, almost impercepti-bly nodding his head as if to say, *Go on, you young fool. Humor this old man. It will cost you nothing.*

After all, what would all this mean to his quest, one day lost? Adams decided to accept the old man's appoint-ment if for no other reason than to satisfy his curiosity.

He heaved a rather audible sigh.

"Very well, sir. I shall join you today. When will we be leaving?"

"We shall depart at half eight. In the meantime, we will withdraw for our morning meditation."

Then, with a great flourish, His Excellency Norton I, Emperor of the United States of America and Protector of Mexico, arose from the breakfast table, gave one final windowpane-rattling belch, drew himself up to his full height, and grandly departed the dining room with the dignity and grace of a schooner under full sail.

*   *   *

After a rather contentious meeting with the emperor's tailor, the emperor and Adams proceeded to the offices of the *San Francisco Herald*, where the emperor delivered his latest proclamation to his friend, the columnist Samuel Clemens.

"Well, Joshua, what say you and your associate to a bit of lunch at the Rite Spot Saloon about now? It is lunchtime, and I could use some company."

Adams guessed that Clemens and the emperor must be close friends, as Clemens called him by what must be his Christian name, Joshua.

Norton's affect brightened.

"Splendid idea, Sam! Colonel Adams here will be joining us, with your gracious permission."

"Of course he shall, and Adolphus may even spare a scrap or two for your mastiffs."

Adams thought he detected a twinkle in Clemens's eye when the man turned to the former captain—now colonel—and spoke.

"The Rite Spot is a block or so east on Merchant, and we'd better get going if we are to find a seat. They are quite busy this time of day."

The three men and two "mastiffs" exited the *Herald* offices and began walking up Merchant Street. Norton and his dogs led the way, with Adams and Clemens following a half dozen paces or so behind.

Adams spoke to Clemens in a low voice.

"I am astounded that almost everyone that we have encountered this morning—except for that tailor—has been so exceptionally kind toward the emperor and gracious enough not to point out that he is obviously delusional. I find that to be a most generous display of human kindness and tolerance. After what I have seen for the past four years, this acceptance of Norton's hallucination is a welcome sight."

"Yep. The folks here are of a live-and-let-live frame of mind for the most part. Occasionally you may run into a carbuncle like the tailor."

Arriving at their destination, Clemens moved ahead and opened the door to the saloon.

"This is the Rite Spot. After you, gentlemen."

Norton was the first to enter, gesturing grandly to the bartender and patrons, followed by Adams, Clemens, and the two dogs.

"Greetings, Adolphus. We desire a table for lunch, if you please. If there may be a scrap or two extra from the kitchen, we are certain that Lazarus and Bummer would be more than grateful."

Adolphus gave a halfhearted salute.

"Afternoon, Emperor. Lemme clear off a table in the back."

The bartender, holding a disreputable-looking bar cloth in his hand, walked from behind the bar, sporting an apron that had more than likely not seen soap and water since the shelling of Fort Sumter, and ushered the emperor's party to a table in the back, pulling out a chair for the emperor to seat himself. Norton nodded in appreciation and handed the man a fifty-cent promissory note.

"Thank you, Adolphus, our friend and loyal subject."

"Thanks to yerself, sir."

Adolphus turned and headed back toward the bar, returning shortly with three schooners of beer.

"Fish stew terday, yer worship. I'll get 'er right up."

"Thank you, good sir," came the reply from Norton, who then turned to Adams and spoke, sotto voce.

"It's fish stew near every day, Colonel. But no matter, as it is a hearty and filling broth."

After a few minutes, three bowls of fish stew arrived, along with a ham bone and some kitchen scraps for the dogs. In between bites, Clemens and the emperor were involved in a conversation regarding the current state of the city.

"We are remarkably pleased with the cleanliness of the streets this morning, Sam, and the police have been reminded of the respect due their emperor. The constables drew themselves to attention and saluted when we passed them on the street. It is apparent to us that Chief Crowley has corrected the young constable that mistook us for another person and imprisoned us briefly."

"Yep, Joshua. The chief has personally reprimanded the young officer and has issued a directive to his patrol to pay their respects to you in the proper manner."

The emperor was pleased.

"We shall issue a formal pardon to the young offender within the week."

The emperor turned and addressed his colonel.

"We can see that you are somewhat puzzled by the informalities exchanged between Sam and ourselves. Sam is counselor to the realm and a close personal confidant. He and he alone has been granted the prerogative to address us by our Christian name."

There was that mischievous twinkle in Clemens's eye again.

"A signal honor, Joshua. One which I do not take lightly."

The emperor nodded in agreement, then got up from the table. Adams braced himself for one of Norton's prodigious belches that he had recently experienced at breakfast.

The colonel was not disappointed.

"It is time for our afternoon meditation. We shall not be needing you for the rest of the day, Colonel Adams."

The Emperor then abruptly turned toward the door and left. Lazarus and Bummer, ever loyal to the old man, abandoned their ham bones and trotted out behind him.

"Well, Cap'n, what say we return to the newspaper and talk a bit?"

Adams nodded in agreement.
"Thanks, I'd like that. What is my share of the meal today?"

"There is no charge. The proprietor of the Rite Spot has taken care of our bill. Restaurant owners throughout the city have made the emperor a bit of a celebrity, and he dines at no charge in the finest establishments in the city. Many of them have brass "By Appointment of his Majesty Emperor Norton I" plaques posted at the entrance to their dining areas. They get the notoriety and exposure to tourists, and he gets his dinner."

"Astounding! I wondered how this man fed himself. And his room rent?"

Clemens smiled.

"Paid for by the local Masonic lodge, clothing paid for by the City Board of Supervisors. Mr. Norton is a genuine tourist attraction for us here and is a gentle and harmless sort in the bargain. Our emperor is much loved—or at least tolerated—in our city and in many instances is a boon to local commerce."

* * *

The Mountain Man

Mulligan's Carson City Saloon and Casino was in full swing that Thursday evening when Jeb Ford pushed open the doors and walked inside. The poker and roulette tables were filled with all manner of miners, woodsmen, sharpers, and townsfolk hoping to win a few dollars or more at the gaming tables, and the patrons were two deep at the bar. The smell of stale sweat permeated the casino, and a heavy tobacco-smoke haze enveloped the entire front of the large building. Mulligan's hostesses were busily working the tables, some as dealers or croupiers, others busily cadging overpriced drinks from the miners who had come to town for a little excitement. Those men who wished a short time with a hostess were taken upstairs to one of the rooms that were available for that purpose.

Ford walked wearily through the casino to the rear of the building and sat down at a table. He was interested in only a meal and perhaps a whiskey or two. The old mountain man had come down to try his hand at prospecting after his squaw had died four months previously, and he'd had little success to show for the effort. *Another month of this*, he thought, *and then if it don't pan out, I'll see about scouting for the Army garrison up at Fort Hall.*

Ford was fifty-four years old and was among the most respected scouts and guides in the west. He had scouted, trapped, and fought hostile Indians for more than thirty-five years alongside the legendary scouts Kit Carson and Jim Bridger and had the regard of all who knew him. He was a large and powerful man, virtually fearless, and in possession of a sense of honor and dignity that one rarely saw in the west. Neither a bully nor a braggart, Ford was a quiet man who would go out of his way to avoid a quarrel, but should one be unavoidable, woe betide the man or men who provoked him.

The old scout had been seated at his table for a few minutes when John Mulligan came over to greet him.

"Evenin', Jeb. How's it going at your stake these days? Sloughed any ore lately?"

"A considerable amount of mud and rock is 'bout the sum total of it, John. Haven't seen anything in weeks."

Mulligan sat down at Ford's table and motioned to one of the hostesses to bring a bottle and two glasses.

"Well, let me help you take some of the creak from those bones. Let's have a whiskey or two before you eat. My bottle."

"Mighty generous of you, John. Don't mind if I do."

The bottle arrived, and Mulligan poured two shots of his personal reserve bourbon into each glass.

"Good health, Jeb. Put that behind your necktie."

"Good health, John. My, that goes down smooth."

Mulligan smiled.

"Yep. Have it shipped in from Tennessee for my own personal use. No whiskey drummer ever sold anything as smooth as this."

"No argument there, John. Don't believe I ever had any such before."

Mulligan poured two more doubles into the glasses, and the men drained the shots in one neat throw.

"What'll it be tonight, Jeb? The usual stew, or something else?"

Ford thought for a moment and then answered.

"John, I think tonight I'll have one of those steaks and some boiled potatoes and wash it down with a beer or two."

Mulligan motioned to one of the hostesses nearby, who promptly came over to the table.

"The cow's hind side it is. Emma, Jeb here is having steak and spuds tonight. And a schooner of beer to wash it down, please."

Emma nodded and smiled shyly at the mountain man.

"Evening, Mr. Ford. I'll get this right in. You like it rare, don'cha?"

Ford smiled at the pretty, plumpish young woman.

"Believe I do, Emma, thank you."

Emma giggled, turned for the kitchen, and left with Ford's food order.

"You know, Jeb, I do believe that Emma has an eye for you. She's a good girl, you know. Not like the whores that work here. Emma just comes to work and waits on the customers and then goes to her room. Sturdy and hard-working. You could do a damn sight worse than have Emma warmin' your bed."

Ford gave a short laugh in that dismissive way he affected whenever the subject of finding a replacement for his squaw came up.

"John, I ain't slept in a bed not more'n ten times in the last thirty years. And whenever I did, I had the back miseries for a week after. Just a bedroll and a place to throw it'll be all I'm needin'."

Ford continued.

"No, sir, I reckon that I ain't fancied a white woman in years. If I do decide to marry agin...which I ain't...it'll be an Arapaho squaw who can live the life of the mountains. I have little time or regard for the niceties of civilized living."

Mulligan was about to respond when the sound of a commotion came from the bar. Two men were arguing, one quite loudly, the other responding in a calm and level voice.

"Shit. Better see what this is all about. Excuse me, Jeb, be back shortly."

Mulligan got up from the table, walked over to the end of the bar, retrieved a bung starter from a shelf on the bar back, and walked over to the two men having the argument.

"Henry Cherry! Might have known. Didn't I bar you out of here last week?"

Cherry turned and stared at John Mulligan. His face was beet red and his eyes were bulging.

"You stay the fuck outta this, John Mulligan, or you'll get some of what I'm fixin' to give this snot-nosed, baby-faced bastard here."

Mulligan didn't say a word in response but swiftly made a half turn to his right, wheeled, and delivered a bone-crushing blow with the mallet to Cherry's left knee.

Cherry dropped to one knee like he was shot, howling in pain.

"My knee! You busted my knee, you Mick son of a bitch. I'll kill you."

As Cherry reached clumsily for his revolver, Mulligan bent slightly at the waist and delivered another blow with the mallet, this time to Cherry's skull.

Cherry's eyes rolled up into his head, and he collapsed on the floor. The sickening crack of mallet on bone had done its work. Cherry was out cold, possibly suffering a fractured skull.

Mulligan turned to the man with whom Cherry had been arguing.

"Well, Tom Adams! Having a bit of employee-management difficulties here?"

Adams nodded in the affirmative.

"And it has apparently been settled, I would say. You haven't killed the man, have you?"

"Wasn't for not trying, Tom. I run a friendly place here, a place where hardworking men can come and relax and have a good time. I will not tolerate any disruption or unpleasantness in my establishment. You cannot argue or dialogue with men like Cherry. You can only remove them as quickly and forcefully as possible and disabuse them of any thought of retaliation. Which reminds me..."

Mulligan kneeled over Cherry's prostrate form and spread Cherry's right hand out on the wooden floor. After raising the mallet above his head, Mulligan brought it down, delivering a shattering blow to Cherry's gun hand.

Cherry, in a near coma, moaned.

"If Mr. Cherry decides to settle the score in the future, he'll have to do it left-handed."

Mulligan turned to his two bartenders on duty.

"Pick up Mr. Cherry and remove him from the premises. And if either of you allow someone in here that is barred again, you'll answer to me."

The two barkeeps came out from behind the bar, picked up Cherry's inert body, and unceremoniously dumped him outside on the walkway.

"Come into the restaurant, Tom. There's someone I'd like you to meet. Charlene, bring another whiskey glass to Jeb's table in the back."

Tom Adams and the saloon keeper walked back to the table where Jeb Ford was seated and sat down.

Ford was the first to speak, extending his rough hand to Adams.

"Don't believe we've met, sir. I'm Jeb Ford."

Adams shook hands with the mountain man. His own hand was engulfed by Ford's huge calloused paw.

"Tom Adams. I'm the Wells Fargo express agent here. Pleased to make your acquaintance."

"Howdy, Tom. I see you were involved in a dustup with Henry Cherry out there at the bar. Cherry's a bad one. Can't hold his liquor, gets meaner than a rattlesnake with the piles when he's drunk. He'll shoot you in the back soon as look at you."

"I've only been here a short while," Adams replied, "but I'm damn well familiar with Mr. Cherry's behavior. My predecessor had hired him as a shotgun rider. My lead whip refuses to carry him on his run, and half the time, he was too drunk to work. What you heard out there was my attempt to sever relations between Mr. Cherry and Wells Fargo."

Mulligan interjected,

"Cherry was drunk as usual and was fixing to create a disturbance in my establishment. I won't have such behavior in here. Cherry deserved just what he got, and maybe a little more."

Ford laughed. "Well, nobody's gonna lose any sleep over what happened to him, that's fer certain."

Ford turned his head toward Adams.

"Tom, you'd better keep a weather eye toward Henry Cherry. He's a shifty, drunken coward who will be looking to settle up with you down the road. He won't bother with John here because he's yellow. He'll figure that what with you being so young, you'll be easier to take. He'll try and back-shoot you, sure as hell."

Adams nodded.

"Well, Mr. Cherry is welcome to try. He may find that I'm not as easy to ambush as he thinks. He isn't the first, and he more than likely won't be the last. When John came up to the bar, I was attempting to get Cherry out of the saloon and deal with him outside. Looks like he should have done so, what with that bung starter belaboring him about the head."

Mulligan looked at Adams.

"Good advice, Tom. I know that you can handle yourself. Just keep an eye peeled, that's all."

Just then, Emma arrived with Jeb Ford's dinner and a large schooner of beer.

"Here you are, Mr. Ford, sir. Steak's so rare it moved when I stuck it with the serving fork."

"Looks just right to me, Emma. You always know how to take care of me."

Blushing, Emma giggled and shifted uneasily from foot to foot.

"Alright, Emma, bring us another bottle of my bourbon, and then go look after your other customers, dear."

"Yes, sir, Mr. Mulligan. I'll bring it right over."

Emma turned and left the men to their conversation.

Ford began carving away at the large beefsteak on the platter in front of him, taking huge bites of the meat with an accompanying boiled potato and washing the mouthful down with a draught of beer from the schooner.

"Tell you what, John," he said after a few bites, "don't let your cook go off and work somewheres else. This is some tasty grub."

Mulligan nodded in assent and then addressed Tom Adams.

"Tom, Jeb here might just be able to help you some in your—What do you call it?—your quest. Anyways, Jeb and Kit Carson trapped and scouted together back in the day."

Jeb nodded and spoke.

"I have known General Kit Carson more than thirty-odd years. First met him in Santa Fe back in twenty-nine. What are you looking for, Tom?"

Adams could barely contain his excitement.

"I came west to learn of the real Kit Carson and to gather information to construct a book that tells of his true adventures. Dime novels these days have written wildly exaggerated accounts of his life that border on the delusional. I am interested in the factual accounting of first-person descriptions of his many achievements."

Jeb Ford smiled.

"Well, if that is the case, you'll make little progress talking with General Carson. Old Kit is about as closed-mouth a man as I ever met, especially when it comes to his own life and times."

"And you, Jeb? Will you be kind enough to accommodate me? I will be more than happy to offer some payment, but it won't be much, as I don't have a large salary as it is."

Mulligan interposed.

"Jeb, I can tell you that in the short period of time that I have known Tom, here, he has been nothing but a straight shooter and a man of his word. If you should talk to any man, it should be Tom Adams, here."

Ford thought for a moment, then spoke.

"An occasional meal when I happen to be in town will be fine, Tom. Don't need to be paid for my life and times with Kit Carson, as the remembering is payment enough."

Ford continued to speak, adding,

"If you'll take care of John and Emma for tonight's supper, we'll start right now."

Adams beamed.

"Done! Let's have a round to celebrate."

"We'll have it from my bottle," Mulligan said, "and I intend to be at the table for every episode."

Ford thought for a moment, recalling those days of long past, then began his narrative.

"It were eighteen and twenty-nine. I had left Missouri and headed out on the Santa Fe Trail lookin' for work. After some unpleasantness with some Injuns up around Cimarron, I arrived at the trail's end in Santa Fe, where I became acquainted quite by accident with a fellow by the name of Billy Morgan. His older brother Augustus had built a tradin' post up near Taos and had sent for young Billy to construct a redoubt there, as the Utes and Navajo were none too friendly at the time. Augustus believed that once the redoubt was constructed, he could persuade the tribes to engage in commerce and live peaceably with the whites who were trappin' for beaver and huntin' buffalo along the Arkansas and further north."

Tom Adams had hastily pulled a pencil and some scraps of paper from his jacket pocket when Ford began his remembering and was scribbling furiously.

"Gentleman by the name o' Ewing Young had gotten together a trappin' and huntin' party, and as I was a green lad of seventeen and hadn't tried my hand at trappin' or such, Mr. Young hired me on as a cavvy boy to tend the horses and other livestock, so I let Billy know that I'd be winterin' with the trappin' party and wasn't goin' to be workin' on buildin' that redoubt.

"Two days later, I bid adios to Billy Morgan and Santa Fe, which I didn't much like, anyways, and headed north with Ewing Young's trappers.

"One of the scouts for that expedition was Kit Carson, him being two year older than I, but it was generally known that Kit were the sharpest-eyed scout in the party and maybe in all the southwest territories.

"Ol' Kit never once kept his eyes in one spot for very long and never allowed hisself to be distracted from that which he was paid to do, namely find water for the party and to stay vigilant for any sign of hostile tribes."

Adams was writing down Ford's story as fast as he knew how. He noticed that Ford had lapsed into some of the vernacular that he guessed was from his trapping days some thirty-five years earlier.

Adams said hurriedly, "A moment please, Jeb, while I catch up here."

"Let's have another bourbon," Mulligan said, then refilled the other men's glasses and poured one for himself.

"Don't mind if I do, John," Ford replied. "All this talk can dry out a man's whistle."

Ford took a sip from the refilled bourbon glass and followed it with a draught from the schooner, then continued.

"We left Santa Fe in July of thirty and headed north for Taos. Ewing had a well-armed brigade of some sixty-odd trappers and another fifteen or so of us that were hired at a dollar a day to tend the livestock, cook, and such. Kit had five Paiute scouts with him. Our livestock count were some seventy extra horses, one hundred cattle, and sixty mules, some o' which we intended to trade in Taos for winterin' supplies and some to butcher and use as food for the men.

"Second day out from Santa Fe, Kit comes a-ridin' in with two of his Paiutes and tells Ewing that they have run across a war party of some forty 'r more Utes encamped near the Rio Grande about twenty miles ahead.

"Kit tells Ewing that the war party has pitched camp and has their women and children with 'em. Says they look like they're hungry and he wouldn't be surprised if one of their scouts had already spotted us and that maybe we better lay out an ambush for any raidin' party comin' down to steal our livestock.

"Well, sir, ol' Ewing Young says that ain't near necessary, as they's prob'ly too weak to mount up a war party worth anything and that we'd just post a normal watch on the herds tonight and send out a skirmish party with Kit in the mornin' to take care of the war party and maybe take a few women and children as prisoners to trade with the Mexicans up Taos way."

Adams was aghast.

"Women and children? Traded as slaves?"

"Yep. Injuns and Mexicans been raidin' each other and takin' their people as slaves for more than two hunnert years. Mostly Navajos, but a few Utes and Jicarillas now and again."

Well, that must have been the way of life here long before I arrived, Adams thought, *and I'll say no more about it.*

Adams, the former cavalry officer, was envisioning Ewing Young's tactic in his mind.

"Jeb, how many men did Ewing Young want for this skirmish party the next day?"

"Not more'n fifteen or twenty, along with Kit and the Paiutes. Come down on 'em a-whoopin' and a-hollerin', scare the bejeezus out of 'em, kill as many warriors as possible, take some women and children, burn their tipis, and get the hell out of there."

Adams remarked on the strategy that had been put forth by Young.

"Well, if you're coming right at them as Ewing Young wanted and you have an inferior force, you'll need the element of surprise if you want to win the day."

Ford nodded in agreement.

"Kit didn't like Ewing's plan at all. He wanted to set an ambush that night while we was camped. He knew that the Utes were near to starvin' and would be comin' in quietly to cut out a dozen or so of the horses to take back to their camp for food. Ewing said no, by God, that he were bankrollin' this trappin' expedition and that he'd make the call on how the herds would be looked after at night."

Ford took another sip of the bourbon and beer, then smiled.

"Ol' Kit, he didn't take to that at all, said he was hired on to scout and that he was well-acquainted with hungry savages and knew what they'd be up to."

Ford continued the narrative, but his remembrance of the tragedy that befell the trapping party that night erased the smile from his face.

"Ewing's face got red as a beet, told Kit that he was runnin' the show and if he didn't like it, he could draw his pay. He said that John Martin would be posted as first watch to the livestock, which were out to graze about fifty yards or so from the main camp. Any trouble, Ewing said, Martin would fire that ol' Tryon muzzle loader of his and we'd be out there, Johnny on the spot.

"Kit didn't say a word after that, but his jawline was set in stone. Just turned away from Ewing and walked off to his saddle and bedroll over by the Paiutes."

Mulligan wanted to know more.

"Jeb, what happened that night? You're not going to leave us hanging there, are you?"

"Not as long as that bottle's on the table, John. We'll keep on going."

Ford took another sip of the bourbon and continued.

"Seemed like the disagreement between Ewing and Kit was settled, although we knew that Kit didn't like it one bit.

"Funny thing about ol' General Carson, when he was given an order, he stuck with it whether he liked it or not. He just wouldn't buck a higher authority. He'd argue his case, and if it didn't go his way, well, then he'd just set his jaw and carry that order out."

Adams, writing as fast as he could interjected..

"Jeb, if Kit felt so strongly about setting the ambush, I would think that he'd go ahead and set it, never mind what Ewing said."

Jeb thought for a moment, then patiently answered.

"Kit Carson could speak half a dozen 'r more Injun languages like he was one of 'em and could make hisself understood in half a dozen more. He spoke Spanish like he was born to it, but he couldn't read nor write English. Never could since he was a shaver. I always thought that this is what held him back from buckin' somebody that could do both. He showed it that night in the dustup with Ewing Young, and I'd be seein' it more as we trapped and scouted in the years to come."

"Sorry for the interruption, Jeb. Please go on."

"About four in the morning, we hear a shot fired out by where the livestock's grazing. Ol' Kit's the first one there, and what does he find? John Martin's throat had been slit from ear to ear and he'd been scalped. Think it was about twenty or so of the horses had been cut out and quietly led off. Nobody ever heard a sound, not even Kit hisself. The feller that was to relieve poor ol' John was Martin's friend Cecil Davis. Cecil found him like that and fired the warning shot.

"Shortly after, Ewing Young arrives and is fit to be tied. Tells Kit that he was right and that Ewing was wrong and it cost the life of a good man.

"Martin's body was cold, so Kit thought that the raiding party had about a four-hour or more head start and once out of earshot would be ridin' hell-bent for leather. Ewing says he won't interfere and that Kit should do whatever it takes to get them horses back, as we'd be needin' 'em for the winter.

"Kit says he'll take fifteen men and the Paiutes and pursue the Ute war party. Then he points to me and says he'll take the cavvy boy too, and can I ride and shoot?

"I'm about to bust my britches for the chance to ride out with Kit Carson, so I tell him Hell yes I can, and just as good as the next man.

"'You'll be gettin' the chance to prove it,' he tells me and then says, 'Grab your gear and cut out a horse, and we're movin' in about ten minutes.'

"I was ready in five. When the raidin' party was ready to go, Kit gathers us up and tells us that he thinks that these Utes is Winniniuc Utes and they'd be headin' northwest into the mesa lands of Utah where their tribal grounds was."

Adams asked a question of Ford.

"Jeb, just how did Kit know which Ute tribe the war party was from?"

"They had tipis in their camp, so Kit reckoned that these were Utes from the southern tribes. The Winniniucs had sent war parties down in twenty-eight, and Kit, he reckoned that this was the same. The tribe was starvin', and war parties were out lookin' for food to get through the winter.

"Anyways, we mounted up and headed off to the northwest towards the Ute tribal lands up by the Colorado. The trail wan't hard to follow; them twenty horses left plenty of tracks. Kit says that we need to spare our mounts, as this was gonna be a long trail and so we'll just go along in a lope and let the Utes think that we ain't followin'."

Ford paused and drained the last of the beer from his schooner. Mulligan motioned to Emma to bring him another from the bar as Ford continued talking.

"We figured we could travel faster than the war party, so we didn't want to run up on 'em—that'd give the Utes the advantage, as they had numbers on us. Kit's plan was to let 'em get feelin' all safe in their territory and then surprise 'em at sunrise one morning—come at 'em with the sun at our backs, kill as many of the warriors as possible, and run the others off, take some women and children, and get the horses back."

Emma arrived with a fresh beer for Ford. Jeb smiled at the blushing waitress, then

nodded at her and winked.

"Thank you, honey."

Emma giggled and walked away.

Ford took a pull from the fresh glass and then continued.

"Now, where was I? Oh.

"Well, Kit reckoned that we'd lose a couple of the horses that the Ute war party would eat along the way, and sure enough, we was about a day out when we came across one of the animals that had been butchered for food. Didn't see no smoke from a campfire, so we reckoned that they just skinned the animal for the hide and took a good bit of the flesh to eat and ate it raw."

Adams had to ask.

"Jeb, what did Kit and the rest of the men in your party think about killing the horse for food?"

"Happens all the time out here, Tom, mostly in winter if'n you run out of game to kill. Done it myself, and so has the general. Horses, mules, don't make any never mind. When you ain't got nothin' to eat, you cut one out and butcher it. Lot of winter- over trappin' expeditions carry extra horses and mules not only for pack but for food if the need happens. We didn't think nothin' of it. We'd just take the Ute horses as replacement for the ones they ate after we killed the warriors."

Mulligan was completely engrossed by Ford's narrative. He asked,

"How far did your party follow the war party?"

"More'n two weeks, clean up into the high desert plateau in southern Utah. We'd been closin' in on 'em little by little, and we found ourselves not four hunnert yards from the war party one night.

"The Utes had set camp in a ravine surrounded on two sides by some high land with a considerable amount of scrub and rock formations. They was pretty sure that nobody had followed 'em from the raid on Ewing's camp, but they was dead wrong, you know.

"They had butchered two of our horses on the trail, and now they was so sure that nobody was behind 'em, they commenced to settin' up camp and buildin' fires to cook the horseflesh that they'd been chewin' on raw while on the trail.

"Well, sir, Kit says, 'Let 'em get their camp set, as they'll be back on their heels just a bit, wantin' to rest some and eat more'n just a strip of raw horseflesh a day. When they get set up and all comfy, we'll descend down on 'em like demons from Hell and massacre 'em.'"

Adams couldn't believe what he had just heard.

"Massacre? You were going to massacre them?"

"In them days, there wan't any rules about gentleman's war. You killed 'em, and as many as you can. Don't make no difference if they's squaws or young'uns; you just give 'em back what they had given you beforehand."

Mulligan agreed with Jeb.

"Tom, you only have to come up on one wagon or home or spread and see what these savages do to women and children. Women is raped and butchered, and the children that ain't taken off are killed and butchered too. Wasn't any niceties back then. I've seen army dragoons that was scalped and their hearts cut out of their chests to be eaten by the bloodthirsty savage that killed them. Some tribes believe that you become—what's the word—not able to be killed."

"Invincible."

"Yep, invincible. Come across that a time or two, and you'll be more than happy to return the favor, and then some."

Adams couldn't believe his ears.

"Jesus!"

"Don't see much of that round here nowadays, but if you was to venture up around the Dakotas in the Black Hills, I expect the same butchery continues, and will continue until the savages is completely bested."

Ford continued with his recollection.

"Anyways, the Ute war party had their camp set by nightfall, and they was going about their business like they wan't a white man within a hunnert miles. We had stayed low all day, no fires and no food, just a little water and some jerky. My job was to manage the horses and keep 'em quiet as possible, which, seein' as I had tended them to start, wasn't much trouble at all. Only worry we had was if the wind shifted and the horses could smell the Ute camp, as that'd make 'em skittish—you know, jumpy, nervous and such.

"Well, the Ute camp bedded down for the night, all comfy in their tipis, and only two or three warriors was awake to watch the horses. As the night became cool, the warriors that was awake wrapped up in their blankets and was kind of, you know, noddin' off now and again. Guess all that food and fire after them bein' hungry for so long cozies 'em up some.

"We stayed shiverin' all night, didn't catch a wink o' sleep. We wanted to be awake and ready to fight come daybreak.

"It must be around two in the morning or so of this long and cold night, and Kit comes around to give us the final word on the raid. The Paiutes was to circle around behind the camp and at first light commence a-howlin' and screamin' and firin' at the camp to cause the Utes to think that the attack was comin' from behind. Then when they was fixin' to head toward all that noise, we'd descend down on em', screamin' and hollerin' and shootin'. Kit figured that the Utes would panic and get the hell out as fast as they could, leavin' the stolen horses behind.

"Well, sir, first light breaks, and the Paiutes mount up and come directly at the camp, screamin' like banshees. Ain't no love lost between the tribes. You'd-a thought that there was a whole war party comin' in. We was mounted up and ready to go, and when Kit heard the Paiutes, he gives the signal to head in."

Ford stopped for a moment, either to catch his breath or to remember the moment precisely. Both Adams and Mulligan were waiting when the old trapper continued the narrative.

"We heard the Paiutes, and we come in the camp in a skirmish line with the mornin' sun at our backs. Kit wanted the skirmish line, as he called it, so that the lead riders wouldn't get shot by accident by one of our boys followin'. I'll tell you, we were makin' some kind of racket comin' in, as if to say, 'Here we come, you Ute bastards. We goin' ta kill every mother's son of you.'

"We caught the Utes back on their heels. They couldn't believe that we'd tracked 'em that far for just a few horses, but ol' Kit was like that. If you took somethin' that he figured belonged to him and his men, he'd track your ass to China if he had to, and when he caught up with you, like as not, he'd kill you for his trouble."

Jeb Ford was in the moment as he recounted the particulars of his first real Indian fight. Eyes narrowed and fists clenched, he continued his narrative.

"There was indiscriminate shootin' from both sides. Some women and boys was hit as the savages began to see that they was set upon from two sides. I was mounted up and firin' quick as I could reload, almost two shots a minute. Ol' Kit and Cecil Davis was hollerin' and firin'—they was the two quickest at reloadin' those old cap-and-ball muzzle loaders, could fire and reload about three times a minute while ridin' at gallop! Kit's first shot took down a warrior that was about to launch an arrow, shot him clean through the nipple and kilt him dead, reloaded and shot another of the warriors off his horse while I was loadin' my second shot.

"Just then I happen to look over at ol' Cecil Davis. Cecil had blood in his eye, what with John Martin bein' his friend and all, and he's a-firin' and loadin' and screamin' somethin' at the top of his lungs—don't know what exactly."

Ford drained his whiskey glass and poured another from the emptying bourbon bottle.

"Then as I'm about to get off another shot, I see ol' Cecil rare back and fall off his horse. I figure, well, ol' Cecil's been kilt for sure, but no, sir, he's up and got his huntin' knife drawn and headin' straight for a Ute warrior on horseback, takes one swipe and guts the horse. The Ute warrior falls with the horse and his leg's pinned underneath, cain't move, see? Cecil goes up to him and slits his throat and then in the middle of the fray ups and scalps the savage like he's got all the time in the world.

"I figured when Cecil fell off his horse that he was shot and maybe dead, but he sure wasn't actin' like he was. He was fightin' the Utes like a madman, kilt three or four of 'em by hisself."

Adams posed a question.

"Jeb, how long did the battle go on? A day or more?"

Ford snorted.

"It was over in an hour. Took 'em by complete surprise, we did. Kilt nine of the warriors. Couple of squaws and boys were caught in the crossfire, and the rest hightailed it out in all directions. Left all their tipis and blankets and such behind, and three of their squaws that couldn't find a horse in time to mount up and hightail it out. One was a Mexican gal that had been taken in a raid, she reckoned it was back in twenty-five. She had been with the Utes long enough that we didn't trust her no more'n we did the other two."

Adams looked up from his notes to ask the mountain man another question.

"How many in your party were casualties?"

Ford fell quiet for a moment, reflecting on the aftermath of the battle.

"Two of the Paiutes—Bill Always-Wears-Hat and another one, can't exackly remember who he was—and one of our boys, Randall Maker, were all hit by arrows in the chest and gut and kilt. Cecil had been shot in the chest, but turns out that the Utes was short on black powder for their old flintlock muzzle loaders and the shot didn't have enough powder charge to do anything. That musket ball barely broke his skin and stuck there. When everything had calmed down, Kit walked over to ol' Cecil and just picked that musket ball off of his skin just as nice as you please. Everybody got a good laugh on that.

"Kit sent me and two others in our party—can't rightly remember who—to round up the horses and bring 'em in. That took a couple hours. When we got back, they were just finishin' buryin' Randall and the Paiutes and burnin' the Ute camp.

"We scalped the dead Utes and tied their scalps to our saddle horns with rawhde and tied the women up on three of the horses. We reckoned that once the Utes figured out how many was in our raid party, they'd be a-lookin' for us, so Kit wanted to head south and hightail it for Taos right now.

"Turns out that the Ute that Cecil went after with his Bowie knife had John Martin's scalp tied to his lance. Cecil seen that blond scalp, and musket ball or no, he went for him and scalped him in the middle of the fight.

"We headed southeast on a gallop and stopped only to rest a bit now and then and change horses and was back in eight days and met up with Ewing and the rest of the trapping expedition."

*　　*　　*

Shunar

October 13th

My arrival in Carson City has been celebrated by the gods of weather with the gift of a sudden and all but crippling storm that has left the transport of persons and goods temporarily immobilized. Some of the old-timers here opine that things will resume a semblance of normality shortly, however at the time of this journal entry we remain stalled.

On a more positive note I have retained the trapper and mountain man Jeb Ford as our security consultant and armed guard. As he has a vast knowledge of the mountains and I'm certain that he'll be an asset to our office, providing I can persuade him to stay with us and not return north to the Rockies where he longs to be. Mr. Ford has little love for civilized living, or foofaraw, as he so succinctly calls the trappings of town life.

*   *   *

A week had passed since the early winter storm had all but buried the trails leading to and from Carson City. Commerce had slowly returned as the trails had become passable. Work had begun on the temporary telegraph end pole for Al Mudd's Western Union office that would tap into the transcontinental line feed just outside of the town. The stage routes were open, and travel had been resumed on a scaled-down winter schedule. Freight wagons were routinely making the trip to the rail head in Reno, and supplies were arriving daily.

Jeb Ford, working for Wells Fargo as a security consultant, had remained in Carson City, securing a small space in the back of the stable where Wells Fargo kept their wagon teams. He had been mostly utilized as an armed scout on the mountain-crossing runs to detect any unusual signs of renegade Paiutes or outlaws. Since Ford's hire as a scout, there had been no attempts to waylay the Wells Fargo rolling stock, nor had he detected any recent signs of unusual activity along the routes.

Tom Adams locked the door to his Wells Fargo office on the evening of October 20 and walked briskly toward John Mulligan's saloon. The skies were clear, and there wasn't a breath of wind to be detected. The air was biting cold, the sort of cold that would hurt a man's lungs if too deep a breath were taken. The sole thought in Adams's mind that evening was of a hot meal and a steaming mug of John Mulligan's strong black coffee.

It was Friday, and the patrons were two deep at the bar. The gaming tables were at full capacity.

Adams walked through the bar and gaming room to the restaurant in the rear, which was also enjoying a brisk trade. Looking around the room, he saw John Mulligan and Jeb Ford seated at Mulligan's reserved corner table and walked over to join them.

"Evening, John. Evening, Jeb. John, I see that the cold weather has had little effect on your front-room business."

"Mostly the timber crews out there tonight, Tom. Don't know why, as they're not supposed to be paid until first of next month, but they're out there now having a grand old time. Not that I'm complaining, mind you."

Smiling, Adams turned to Jeb.

"Jeb, how's things going with you? Any sign of trouble on that trail running through the mountains west of here?"

"Ain't seen any new signs of Al White Feather's party. They're prob'ly further up the timberline, but my guess is they're runnin' short of food and ammunition, what with all this early snow, and might be gettin' a mite itchy to ambush some of these settlers crossin' to California. Wouldn't be surprised if it was gonna happen sooner than later."

Mulligan nodded in the direction of an empty chair.

"Sit down and join us, Tom. We're just about to have a bit of supper and perhaps a whiskey or two."

"Thanks, John, I will, but if you don't mind, I'll be having coffee instead of whiskey."

Mulligan and Ford both laughed.

"No offense taken, Tom. Let's see if we can get Emma's eye to take our dinner order. Looks like a banner night out front, so, boys, dinner's on me!"

"Thank you kindly, John," Jeb said. "I'll prob'ly get the elk stew tonight. Looks mighty good."

"Think I'll have the same, Jeb," Adams agreed. "Sounds good to me too."

Mulligan motioned to Emma who, seeing that Jeb Ford was sitting at the table, rushed over to take the three men's dinner order.

"Evenin', Mr. Mulligan, Jeb, Tom. Want something from the kitchen tonight?"

Emma was speaking to Mulligan, but she was looking at Jeb Ford. She had a schoolgirl-crush look on her face.

Jeb Ford, hardy mountain man, trapper, scout, and feared Indian fighter, looked as if he were sitting on a bed of snakes. He looked away from the waitress and focused on Mulligan, who was giving Emma the food order.

"Elk stew all around tonight, Emma, and bring a bottle of my special stock to the table and two glasses. Mr. Adams here will have black coffee."

"Right away, Mr. Mulligan."

Emma turned while giving Ford one last adoring glance and headed for the bar to get John Mulligan's bourbon.

"I swear, Jeb, that sweet young child would love for you to park your boots under her bed. Why don't you take her up on it? Could do a lot worse, you know."

"John, I'll tell you. Come spring, I'm headin' up to Fort Hall to see about scoutin' for the Army there, and I won't be wantin' to worry 'bout some young round-eyed child back here. Besides, if the Army don't want me, I'll be headin' back to the Rockies, and that ain't no place fer a innocent such as her."

"Fair enough, but I say she'd gladly spend time with you this winter if you'd take her up on it."

Tom knew that it was time to change the subject.

"Jeb, as winter progresses, do you think that Wells Fargo will have any problem with this White Feather and his renegades?"

"Like as not we will. Don't think he'll bother with the payroll wagons, as we've too heavy guarded them, but the stage from Placerville might be a worry, and maybe some of the supply wagons. Like I said, they'll be close to starvin' up yonder, and that'll make 'em just a bit more dangerous."

"What does the sheriff have to say about it? Have you spoken with him about this?"

"Yep. He don't want no part of it. Says he's the sheriff and he don't have no juris... juris..."

"Jurisdiction."

"Thanks. Jurisdiction up there. Says it's somethin' the Army needs to take care of."

Emma returned, bringing the whiskey, two glasses, and Adams's coffee on her tray.

"Stew's comin' right up, gents. Mr. Mulligan, do you all want some flatbread with it?"

"That'd be fine, Emma. Now run along before Mr. Ford gets to squirming again."

Emma giggled. "Yes, sir."

Adams broke what was becoming an uncomfortable silence.

"Jeb, from what you have said in the past, you have had great experience in dealing with war parties and renegades. Do you think that Wells Fargo can handle the situation, or do we need help?"

"We ain't got enough men here to go after White Feather. We'd leave everythin' else unguarded. I'm thinkin' that if the Paiute massacre another settler wagon train, the Army'll have to go up there and flush him out. Question is, what kind of Injun sense does they have? I seen some of these youngsters they give a company to cain't find the side of a barn if they was in it."

"Agreed. Well, for the time being, let your guards know to be alert at all times for signs of the renegades. You'll have to figure out which trip your scouting skill is most needed on and take action accordingly."

"Yep. I'll take care of it. Prob'ly git out there and have a look around tomorrow. Placerville run is the one I reckon is most likely to be trouble, what with the trail runnin' through the timberline, and all. Maybe some of the logger camps up yonder, but that ain't our worry unless White Feather's bunch take one of our wagons up there."

When Emma arrived with three bowls of hot, rich, and meaty elk stew, all conversation regarding renegades came to a halt and the three men began devouring the delicious preparation. Mulligan and Jeb Ford had two bowls, but Adams was satisfied after one serving.

Once the meal was finished, Jeb leaned back in his chair, retrieved his old clay pipe and tobacco from his coat pocket, and began to smoke, taking deep draws and inhaling each draw, then allowing the exhaled pipe smoke to leisurely exit through his nose and mouth. Mulligan lit one of his little cigars and drew heavily on it. Adams, a non-smoker, reached into his coat pocket and withdrew some sheets of paper and a pencil.

"I reckon that you're wantin' some more of the wild and woolly tales 'bout trappin' and such. Don't know what you're gonna do with all that, anyway. Don't seem like much to me."

"Jeb, let me see if I can explain it properly. I'm compiling an oral history of the life of you mountain men and trappers. Most of what is read back east is nothing more than dime-store fabrications that tell of wildly exaggerated heroic feats. I want to set the record straight with factual accounting of men like Kit Carson, you, and Jim Bridger. I think that those that come after us deserve to know the real story, don't you?"

"Fine with me, Tom, but I don't see how any of them eastern folk would care much about what happened back then. If it's what you want to do, we'll have at it. Where you want me to start tonight?"

"When you were last in town, you were telling us about Kit's battle with the numerically superior Crow war party. What happened after you returned to Fitzpatrick s camp?"

"Wan't too much longer after we got back with the horses and mules that Galt comes back from Green River with supplies and more traps fer the winter trappin' season. We had plenty o' buffalo and elk meat, and we set to our work of trappin' beaver and guardin' our pelts that we had already trapped and skint. Was good trappin' up there on the Sweetwater that winter, and by the time we was ready to quit the winter quarters, we had plenty o' pelts— nice fat ones that'd fetch a nice price at the Green River meetin' in summer.

"Fitzpatrick had us secure the pelts so other men wouldn't find 'em and steal 'em before we could git to Green River Valley. We reached the south fork of the Platte and bivouacked for the next day or two to see if there was any sign of beaver, that area havin' been trapped near clean.

"Mornin' of the second day, we discovered that two of our party had deserted the day before. Fitzpatrick suspicioned thievery and sent me and Kit to bring 'em back. We never did catch up to the two, as they had a full-day head start on us.

"We reached the site of our winter camp where we had secured several hunnert pounds of pelt, only to find that them two had raised 'em and loaded 'em up on a raft that we had built previously for such a purpose.

"Them two was never heard from again, nor was the pelts ever discovered. Best I could figure was they met up with some Blackfoot who deprived them of their pelts and their hair. Good riddance to 'em, we said. Such men wan't worth nothin' to our small brigade.

"By the time early summer was on us, we'd trapped all the way up to the Snake and it was time to head back and pick up the pelts we'd secured and head for the trade at the Green River Basin, which wan't that far that year, just down in the southwest of Wyoming.

"Them tradin' meets was a sight for a trapper's weary bones. More'n five hunnert trappers from Canada and the west, Tradin' companies outta Saint Louis, Injuns from a dozen or more tribes—Blackfoot, Ute, Arapaho, Bannock, Crow—you name 'em, and they'd be there tradin', playin' games, gamblin', drinkin', and havin' a fine old time. I do miss them meets, I'll say."

"Jeb, weren't there any hostilities among the tribes that were enemies?"

"At these meetin's, there was always a blanket truce among the tribes. They'd trade and play games and smoke, and when it was done, they'd go back to countin' coup on they enemies.

"There was some danger involved time to time, what with all that rotgut whiskey that the fur traders and whiskey drummers had brought in. One year, a trapper were drunker'n ten redskins and was bit by a distempered wolf come close to his camp. Commenced to frothin' at the mouth and rollin' around on the ground, then took off on a dead run and we never seen him again. Ol' Kit allowed as the wolf prob'ly got the worst of it, as that trapper had so much of that rotgut whiskey in him.

"We'd sit around the fire smokin' pipe and sippin' whiskey and see who'd tell the biggest whopper, which was usually Ol' Jim Bridger. Kit used to say that if he was sittin' and smokin' in one of them circles, he wouldn't believe Jim Bridger if'n the man asked him a question. Haw!

"Jim'd sit there and tell them easterners from the tradin' companies 'bout the time he set camp on a canyon ridge that was so wide that it took near eight hours for your echo to return after you shouted it. Haw!

"And some of the easterners wan't sure whether to believe ol' Jim or not. Jim'd tell them he'd shout, 'Git up!' bed down for the night, and wake up to his own call the next mornin'. Haw!"

Adams nodded and smiled.

"Does sound like a really good time after all the winter hardships, Jeb."

"Some o' them trappers couldn't hold they whiskey real good, and that caused some problems, time to time. One of the worst that year was a Frenchy trapper with Captain Drip's party by name of Shunar. He were big, strong, and stupid, and a bully in the bargain. He'd get whiskeyed up and go lookin' for trouble. He'd kill you soon as look at you.

"Now, at this here meet that year, there were an Arapaho girl by the name of Singin' Grass who were just about the most beautiful Injun girl I, or anyone else, for that matter, had ever seen. She wouldn't drink nor squaw up with any of the trappers there, as she was with her kin and stayed in the Arapaho camp.

"Ol' Kit, he'd had a rough year or two, trappin' and fightin' Injuns. Fact was, he'd been wounded in his shoulder two years before and it was still givin' him trouble from time to time.

"I think that it were when Kit spied Singin' Grass he decided that it were time to take a wife, and Kit fancied her for the job.

"Seems that Shunar had spied her and fancied makin' her his squaw as well, but Singin' Grass didn't want nothin' to do with that loud, drunken Frenchy, and one night over at the Arapaho camp, she picked Kit over Shunar at a ceremonial dance of some sort.

"This set the Frenchy into a rage, and later, he tried to force hisself on her, but she got away.

The next day, Kit was in our camp, thinkin' 'bout what to do about Shunar, when the Frenchy walks up, drunk as a lord, and says that Americans wan't nothin' but a bunch of schoolboys and that he just might take a switch and switch 'em to show 'em what's what.

"Well, sir, Kit jumps up, all five foot four of him, and says that he's the worst American in the camp and that he won't allow such talk and if he hears any more of it, he'd rip Shunar's guts."

"With that, Shunar lets out a whoop and heads fer his horse 'n rifle. Kit grabs his single-shot pistol and mounts up, headin' for the center of the camp.

"Didn't take long for the whole camp to know there's gonna be a duel between Kit and Shunar, so just 'bout the whole camp shows up on the green to watch.

"What do you know, here comes Shunar ridin' up on his saddled horse, ready for the fight. Shortly after, Kit's there on his horse, but he's ridin' bareback. The two of 'em git so close together that the horses' heads are touchin'.

"Kit lays them ice-blue eyes of his directly on Shunar and says, 'You gonna shoot me with that?'

"Now, Shunar might be a drunken bully, but he's a crack shot, see? He says to Kit, 'No,' and levels his rifle directly at Kit s heart.

"Just as the two of 'em starts to shoot, Shunar's horse was a bit skittish and jerks up some, which makes Shunar's shot miss his target and graze Ol' Kit just under his left ear. If you was to see him today, I reckon you'd still see that damn scar right there.

"Anyhow, Kit's pistol fires at the same time and hits Shunar in the right hand, takes most of the meat off it, along with Shunar's thumb. Ball goes up his arm and comes out just below the elbow. He's screamin' with the pain and all.

"Now, Kit's pistol were a single-shot pistol, so he rides off to get another one, and when he comes back to finish off Shunar, the Frenchy's off his horse, pleadin' for his life, which ain't much to Kit's likin'. Says he ought to die like he was a man.

"Kit levels that second pistol directly at Shunar's head, goin' to plug him between the eyes. Shunar's wailin' and carryin' on somethin' fierce, 'Please don't kill me,' and such.

"Kit held that cocked pistol on Shunar for a long time, then of a sudden uncorks it and tells the Frenchy that he ain't nothin' more than a drunken coward and a bully and Kit wouldn't be wastin' a ball on his sorry backside that day but he better just steer clear or Kit's be liable to have a second thought 'bout it."

Jeb paused for a moment to catch his breath.

Adams exclaimed, "An amazing story! Had that horse not jerked, what do you think would have been the outcome?"

Ford thought about Adams's question and then replied,

"If the Frenchy's horse hadn't jerked, you wouldn't need to be writin' that book."

"Point taken. Once again, Kit seems to have had Lady Luck on his side."

"Yep. That's so. Kit always had luck ridin' with him, but you know he was also the coolest man I ever knew when he was under fire. Just stayed calm as can be. I think it rubbed off some on the men with him in all the Injun fights over the years, and there was many of 'em."

"Jeb, what happened to Shunar? Did the two men ever fight again?"

"Heard sometime after that gangrene set in to Shunar's arm and it kilt him, but that was after we broke camp and headed back north to trap the Snake River, so I don't rightly know."

"Well, then what happened with Singing Grass?"

"Shortly after the fight with Shunar, Kit went over to the Arapaho camp and presented himself to her father, name of Running Around. Asked for permission to wife Singin' Grass."

"Running Around? That was the Arapaho's name?"

"Yep. In his day, he were a powerful scout. The Arapaho warrior scouts used to signal approachin' enemy by goin' to the top of a butte or such and ridin' in circles. That was a signal to the warriors that enemy were near."

"Did he receive permission?"

"Yep. Gave Running Around the agreed bride price—a new rifle and I think some mules. Cain't remember for sure. They was married in a Arapaho ceremony, and they moved into a tipi that the tribe built for the two of 'em. When the ceremony was done, Kit became a full Arapaho."

"Jeb, when Kit went off with his trapping brigades, did his new wife remain with the Arapaho?"

"When it looked as if it were goin' to be real dangerous, Kit had her stay with the tribe, but they was times when she packed up a travois and went right along with him. Kit liked that, said when she were with him, he never came back to his tipi when there wan't hot water for his feet after settin' traps all day in the cold streams.

"Singin' Grass were a good wife to Ol' Kit, and he loved her dearly. Gave him two daughters. Reckon it was around thirty-nine or so she developed the fever and died. The Arapaho was wailin' and pullin' out they hair and such. Kit set his jaw and didn't show no sorrow nor cry at all. Running Around asked Kit why wan't he mournin' his squaw's death.

"Kit said he were cryin' in his heart as is the white man's custom."

*   *   *

The Bear Flaggers

"Last summer rendezvous were in 1840, up where the Green River and Horse Crick come together. Weren't much to that one. Folks back east stopped buyin' beaver hats and such, and the trapper's life were just 'bout done for after that. Most of us that wan't kilt by redskins or bears by then took up as scouts and guides and hunters for the Army surveyors who was dead set on mappin' out the whole damn northwest."

It was the evening of January 3, 1866. Jeb Ford, Tom Adams, and John Mulligan were having a beer in Mulligan's Saloon while Ford was recounting his life as a guide and hunter for the Army surveyors.

"Still had to keep on the watch for Injuns, as they wan't no more friendlier than they was in the trappin' days. Many a mountain man and surveyor parted with their hair whilst drawin' them maps, that's a fact.

"I lost track of Kit after that last meet on the Green River. Said he wanted to go back east for a spell and see his kin and his daughter Adaline. Kit had brought her east the year before, as he wanted her to read and write and such. Left her with one of his sisters, I think it was.

"I had gone over to Fort Bridger and was doin' some huntin' and guidin' for the Army up around the Snake River. It were alright, but I was gettin' the itch to move on... 'bout like I am these days."

"Jeb, I certainly hope that you can hold off scratching that itch for another few months."

Jeb smiled and took a sip of his beer.

"Just have to see how it plays out, Tom. Like to get back up to Big Sky afore too long."

Adams nodded his head in agreement. He knew better than to press the issue.

"Anyhow, Kit come through Fort Bridger with Captain John Fremont again in April of forty-six with an expedition brigade of some fifty 'r more men. Said they was goin' to map the eastern slope of the Rockies, but seemed to me that they was a lot more men in the expedition than they'd need for just measurin' them mountains."

"That does seem to be a rather large force just for topographical measurements. What was the real purpose of the expedition?"

"We was nowhere near where Fremont was supposed to be goin', and Kit said that we was headin' out along Lansford Hastings's route to the Great Salt Lake. From there we was headin' into California."

"What year was this again, Jeb?"

"Eighteen and forty-six, Tom."

Adams seemed puzzled.

"That was still the sovereign country of Mexico in forty-six, Jeb. Why was Fremont going there?"

"Cain't rightly say I knowed exactly why he was goin' there at the time or who told him he could. Alls I can tell you is that's where we was headin'.

"Well, we get to Salt Lake in 'bout ten days 'r so, and Fremont sees a desert badland ahead and says that we're headin' thataway through that desert and pick up Hastings's trail to the Humboldt River in Nevada. Up where we was last year huntin' Al White Feather's renegades, Tom.

"Well, sir, Fremont and Kit smoke with some of the local Injuns and asks 'bout the badland ahead, and the

Injuns tell Fremont that no white man nor mule ever made it across there alive, accordin' to what they knew.

"Now, don't misunderstand. John Fremont is as brave a man as I have known. Problem is his head was as hard as the melted rocks on the floor of that badland.

"What do you call 'em, Tom?"

"Lava. They are called lava formations, Jeb. Probably thousands of years in the making."

"Yep. Lava. Injuns called that badland a malpais, 'r somethin' like it. They say if you try, you will prob'ly die, and the animals with you.

"Soon as Fremont hears that, he says, 'Well, that's where we're a-goin' tomorrow mornin', first light.'

"And just as sure as God made the moon, we was out on that oven the next mornin'."

John Mulligan interrupted Ford's narrative.

"I'm thirsty just listenin' to this."

Mulligan made a motion to Emma to bring more beer from the bar.

Ford concurred. "Good idea, John.

"Anyways, we get a-goin' out there, and by nine in the mornin', it's already hotter than the blazes of Hell. Off in the distance they's a mountain, but you couldn't tell if it's ten miles away 'r a hunnert.

"It's too hot for a quick pace, it'd wear out the animals, so by that evenin', we'd come 'bout forty miles, mebbe some less, water's runnin' low, animals are 'bout give out, and that damn mountain is still way off in the distance.

"Fremont is thinkin' he mighta bit off a little more than he can chew, so he tells Kit to ride ahead to look for water and grazin' grass while we bedded down on that damned hard rock for the night.

"Plan was that when he found some water, he'd likely have enough grazin' and wood near it to build a bonfire and we'd see it and head thataway.

"Next day, we're out again, lookin' for smoke but don't see nothin' 'til 'bout midafternoon when Basil Lajeunesse points over yonder by one o' them mountains that don't never seem to get no closer, and if you look real hard, you can see a wisp o' smoke risin'."

"Was it Carson?"

"Looked to be 'bout twenty, thirty miles off, Tom. Couldn't say for sure right away if it were him 'r not, but Fremont says that if there's fire, that means that there's somethin' to burn over there and if there's enough to make smoke that far away, there must be water close by, so we're headin' for it."

"And...was it Carson?"

"Yep. Got there in 'bout five hours. Water sure did look good, and there was plenty to graze for the mules. One more day, and we'd a been in real trouble."

Emma arrived with three more schooners of beer.

"Here's your beer, gents. Mr. Ford, you havin' any supper tonight? Stew's real good. Nice and hot."

"That sounds good, honey. Mebbe some flatbread along with it."

"Yes, sir. Comin' right up."

Emma blushed and had turned to take the mountain man's order into the kitchen when John Mulligan spoke.

"Emma, you reckon Tom Adams would like some too?"

Emma s blush escalated into an embarrassed flush.

"Oh! I'm so sorry, Mr. Adams. Are you havin' some tonight too?"

"I believe I will, Emma. Thank you."

"Mr. Mulligan?"

No, Emma, but if you will just bring my bourbon to the table, and some glasses."

"Yes, sir. I'll do that right now."

Emma turned and headed toward the casino-area bar.

"I swear, Jeb, you call that little girl honey, and she forgets she's got a head on top them shoulders. She's real sweet on you for sure."

Jeb ignored Mulligan's observation and picked up his story.

"It was late spring when we got to the Sierra Nevadas, crossed without too much trouble, and then headed north toward the Cascades, where Fremont was pledged to meet some American settlers and a soljer of some sort named Gillespie.

"Fremont sent ten of us ahead to scout and locate this Lieutenant Gillespie's party and guide 'em to Fremont. Me, Kit, Basil, and the Delaware named Denny was amongst the ten.

"We din't have to look too far, as after a day or so, we come across this Gillespie and his men. They'd landed at Yerba Buena in a boat and headed inland lookin' for Fremont.

"Gillespie tells Kit that he has a important message from Washington for Fremont and that he's been travelin' for more'n five months to see him. Says he left Mazatlan by ship disguised as a sailor or somethin' and now he's got to see him—you know, Fremont.

"By now, we was several days from Fremont's party. While headin' to hook up with 'em, we came upon a large camp of Injuns near Tule Lake.

"We talked with 'em and discovered that they was Klamath who had come south to trade for slaves with the

Modocs. We declined an invitation to smoke with 'em, as we considered 'em to be of low character and treacherous, so we pursued our path to meet up with Fremont.

"After a day, we ain't found Fremont, and we camped for the night, as we were weary, having traveled near fifty miles that day. A fire was built, and we wrapped up in our saddle blankets to rest.

"I don't know why we din't set a watch that night. Maybe we was just too tired and din't think that these Klamaths had trailed us lookin' to have our hair.

Anyways, we din't.

"'Bout two, mebbe three, hours after we'd settled in, I hear a pistol shot and ol' Kit's a-yellin', 'Injuns!' and firin' that pistol at what looks to be 'bout fifteen or more redskins. I look over at Basil Lajeunesse and see that he's done got his head tomahawked while he was rolled up asleep.

"Kit said later that it was the sound of the redskin's tomahawk splittin' Basil's head that woke him, what with him bein' a celebrated light sleeper.

"The fight is on, arrows is flyin' everywhere, shots ringin' out, and the moans and death sounds of Injuns fallin'.

"Denny, our Delaware Injun, jumps up, grabs a rifle, and starts firin', but ain't no shots comin' 'cause the damn thing ain't loaded! All you could hear was click, click, and such, and before you know it, Denny falls with five arrows in him. He just gives out a moan and falls dead.

"Our shots find their marks, and several redskins fall, causin' the rest to fade back into the dark cover, but one who I reckon is the war party leader, as his face is the only one painted in war paint, still keeps comin' forward, and him and Kit is locked in a mortal struggle.

"The Injun warrior was among the bravest I ever seen. Had the rest been as brave, we'd all been kilt for sure.

"Me and Gillespie run over to help Kit, and after a bit, the redskin falls, havin' been shot more'n once.

"The fight were done, and we had the advantage.

"Kit and Gillespie see that the brave redskin has a steel axe strapped to his wrist that looked to be British. Kit allows that this is the Injun that kilt Basil while he was asleep. He's grieved that he didn't post a watch, as if he did, ol' Basil'd still be alive.

"Never seen Kit so grieved. He just ripped that steel axe off the Injun's wrist and starts choppin' the Injun's face 'til it ain't nothin' more'n a mess o' pulp.

"He says, 'When the Injuns come to recover the leader, they'll see that his spirit was chopped clean out of his body.'"

Adams, mesmerized by the account of this brief battle of long ago, was puzzled by the arrival of the soldier of some sort, Lieutenant Gillespie.

"Jeb, I'm curious about this Gillespie fellow. Just how—"

His thought was interrupted by Emma, who had brought the stew and flatbread to the table.

"Cain't eat and talk, Tom. Let's dig in."

* * *

The two men, one a lad of barely twenty-three, the other a grizzled trapper, hunter, scout, and Indian fighter in his mid-fifties, ate silently, relishing the hot stew prepared in John Mulligan's saloon kitchen. Mulligan sat patiently waiting for Jeb to continue his epic tale of twenty years past.

"John," Jeb said when he was done, "after more'n thirty years of eatin' mule hide and acorns, I'll tell you that your cook back there is fattenin' me up for the kill. Reckon I ain't worth nothin' to nobody up in Big Sky all fat and lazy like this."

Mulligan laughed.

"Anyhow, this Gillespie feller says he's got a important message for Fremont and we need to get back to him as soon as we can.

"Kit says, 'Well, we'll wait 'til first light and send ol' Jeb Ford over there out to see the whereabouts of them Klamaths, as they might be waitin' to collect up the dead one in our camp, and we'll proceed from there.'

"Gillespie offers to send one o' his marine soljers out with me, but I'd rather have a look alone, as I don't know much about any of these soljers that we come to find."

"Were they waiting to attack again?"

"No, sir, Tom. They had cleared off. Couldn't find nothin' but the trail headin' north. Left the bravest of their lot to the buzzards.

"Told you they was a low sort.

"I get back to our camp and let Kit and the marines know that the Injuns had rode out and were headin' north. Kit and the men had buried our dead in shallow ground under some leaves and rocks, and we packed up and rode south, aimin' to hook up with Fremont and the rest of our expedition."

"Where was Fremont at this time?"

"We reckoned he was at the upper end of the Sacramento Valley, so we headed down there from Tule Lake.

"After two days' steady ride, we come across Fremont down by Sonora. Seems that a mob o' Americans that was livin' in North California up and declared theyselves a independent nation, called theyselves Osos, and announced to all that would hold still long enough to listen that the new country was the Bear Flag Republic, 'r some such nonsense. They wan't no more than a mob, truth be known—stole everything that wan't nailed down, all the horses in town, cleaned out the town armory, threw some of the townsfolk in jail, took the Mexican general—feller by the name of Vallejo—prisoner after drinkin' all his whiskey.

"These Bear Flaggers fancied theyselves a army of liberation, but when I seen 'em, they looked like a collection o' drunkards 'n' thieves. Half of 'em din't have shoes; the other half was drunk after drinkin' up all the Mexican general's whiskey. One of 'em gets aholt of some cloth and draws a bear on it and runs 'er up the town flagpole. Meanwhile, the leader o' this bunch says that we're now in this Bear Flag Republic and that it's Johnny Fremont's duty, as he's an American Army officer, to help these Bear Flaggers defeat the Mexican Army up this way, who is led by this Mexican General Castro.

"I'll tell you, Kit was all for it. He was ready for a good scrap and din't care who it was with. I reckon ol' Kit was still exercised 'bout his friend Lajeunesse. Fremont wan't too sure about the whole mess. Whatever Gillespie told him was in that message caused Fremont to go back and forth 'bout it."

"Jeb, did you ever learn what was in that document from Washington?"

"No, sir, Tom, never did. I was pretty sure it had somethin' to do with where we was, but nobody ever said and Fremont wan't talkin. Only time I ever seen Kit with his nose open 'bout somethin' his superior did 'r din't do.

"Haw. Haw. Told me one night he reckoned that Johnny Fremont got the crack in his ass sittin' astride a fence as a boy.

"Seems this bunch o'...don't rightly know what you'd call em...is planning to move south through the valley over to Monterey on the coast and capture it. Ha! Never heard of such foolishness."

"And? I do know that something transpired, Jeb, as California is part of our United States."

"I'm a-gettin' there, Tom, just hold your horses for a minute whilst I wet my whistle here."

Jeb Ford lifted the schooner of beer and drained it, wiping his mouth on his sleeve in good mountain-man fashion.

"Ever'body was between a rock and a hard place. The Bear Flaggers was led by this feller named Simple or some such. This here Simple knowed he couldn't rightly take Monterey and Santa Barbara without Fremont's help, and ol' Johnny Fremont din't want to move without orders from above sayin' it were alright to move and help the Bear Flaggers.

"So ever'body was sittin' around on their rump, waitin' for somethin' to happen. Bear Flaggers ain't got the army, Fremont ain't got the go-ahead.

"Then somethin' happened that changed the whole shootin' match. This Castro feller sends one of his officers with about a hunnert men or so to retake Sonoma.

"Fremont gets wind of it and says to all within earshot, 'American lives is in jeopardy, boys, and I am now the commander of American Forces in California. We'll move down and reinforce 'em.'

"Din't have far to, go as we was camped 'bout thirty miles 'r so from Sonoma, but by the time we got there, that rag-tag collection o' bandits had run the Mexicans off. I swear I'll never know how that mob did it. Reckon the Mexicans mebbe thought they was more in Sonoma and wan't real keen to scrap.

"Soon as we get there, Fremont promotes himself to major, Gillespie to captain, and Kit and me to lieutenant, says he is now Oso Number One and gussies hisself up with a fancy hat and uniform. He starts givin' orders right and left says anybody that disagrees with his orders is to be thrown in jail and such.

"Kit and me, we din't cotton to that business much. We'd near froze and starved with this man more 'n once, and now he was gettin' high hat with us. I was for headin' back up Fort Hall way, but Kit says, 'Jeb, we been side by side for many a hard time. Stay with me, and let's see where it takes us.'

"I allowed how, seein's it's Kit, I'd stay at least through the march to Monterey, which we was preparin' for, and one week or so later, we was on the march with ol' Oso One up front all dressed out an' on parade. We was pickin' up volunteers along the way to Monterey, and pretty soon, we had a battalion of 'bout a hunnert an' fifty Americans. I was glad to see this army grow, as I din't know what we'd find over at Monterey."

"And? What did you find? Castro's army waiting for you?"

"Nope. We found what looked to be the whole damn American Navy in the harbor and our American flag flyin' from the highest flagpole.

"Seems like we was at war with Mexico after all."

* * *

Al White Feather's Reward

The desert sunset had introduced the two men to a clear, cold, and cloudless night sky. Jeb Ford and Tom Adams had made a small fire for warmth while they waited for Major Twitchell's company to join them. The plan was to rest for several hours and then move out across Forty Mile Desert, heading northwest for Pyramid Lake. Jeb Ford had reckoned that the Indian renegades would make camp there for a few days to rest, which would bring the pursuers closer to their objective. Major Twitchell and Adams saw no reason not to follow his plan. After all, Ford was the experienced tracker that the Army had needed for this mission. To ignore his advice would be folly, a fool's errand.

Shortly after sunset, the cavalry arrived at Adams and Ford's campfire.

"Any trouble finding us, Major?"

"No, Mr. Adams, not at all. We just headed in the direction of a gunshot that we heard and figured that it was you. As we got closer, we saw your fire in the distance."

Adams showed Twitchell the swatch of cloth that had been found.

"This is the same pattern as the dress in the photograph that we found. Looks like we're on the right trail."

"Excellent! Mr. Ford, when do you suggest we ride out?"

"Let's get the horses rested up good for the crossing. If we leave around two, we'll be across by sunup."

"Very well, then. Sergeant Mulhauser, we'll rest here until 0200 hours and continue the pursuit at that time."

"Sir."

"After you have seen to that, return, and we will plan our move across."

"Sir."

The first sergeant left the fire to give the order to bivouac and set the guard and, having detailed Corporal Forrest to execute the order, returned to the fire.

"Major, heading out at 0200 in the morning will give the horses plenty of rest for the crossing. Only take 'bout three or four hours to get across and 'bout another hour to reach Pyramid Lake. When we get to the other side here, I'll scout ahead to see what I can pick up."

Ford continued.

"Once across, it might not hurt to rest 'em up again for a bit. I'll come back and let you know if there has been any movement by the renegades."

Ford got up from the fire and went for his horse.

"Plenty of moonlight tonight. Reckon I'll ride out a ways and look around."

"Right. When will you return?"

"Dunno. 'Bout an hour or two, I reckon, Major"

"Good hunting, Jeb."

"Yep. See you in a bit, Tom."

Ford mounted up and left the camp at a lope.

"Mr. Adams, how on earth does a man of Jeb Ford's years muster up the stamina required to ride all day and then, after only an hour or two by the fire, mount up and ride out to scout the terrain? We'll be on the move again shortly after he returns."

"Tom. Please call me Tom. To answer your question, Major, I don't rightly know. I do know that he spent more than twenty years trapping and scouting with Kit Carson and is a veteran of countless battles with various Indian tribes. I guess that when you live a life in the mountains with the specter of violent death imminent, sleep becomes a luxury. This expedition so far is nothing compared with some of the exploits that he has shared with me. Should we run upon Al White Feather, I expect that I'll be more than happy to have a man like Jeb Ford fighting on my side."

"I keep hearing about this White Feather. Do you think that White Feather is who we are pursuing?"

"Just before your return to our office, Jeb had been scouting the timberline for signs of a renegade Paiute named Al White Feather that had been attacking settler trains and single wagons. Jeb had tracked his renegade band north in the direction of Pyramid Lake. Your accounting of the Reed massacre coincided with White Feather's movements, which leads us to believe that he is the party responsible for Reed's murder and Mrs. Reed's abduction.

"Jeb thinks White Feather is headed back to Bannock tribal country in Wyoming or Idaho, where he'll find safe haven."

Major Twitchell was puzzled.

"Wait. I'm confused. If this White Feather is a Paiute, why are he and his party headed for Bannock territory?"

"The Bannock are a Northern Paiute tribe who are more troublesome than most Paiute clans nowadays. Jeb has a strong suspicion that White Feather and his renegades are Bannock Paiutes come south to raid the wagons on the Overland Trail."

Twitchell nodded.

"By God, when we find him...and we will find him...he'll be made to pay for his butchery. Justice will be swift and final."

Adams debated for a moment whether or not to question Major Twitchell as to the meaning of his last statement but decided to let it alone.

"Well, Major, I believe I'll get a few hours' shut-eye. I can't keep up with Jeb Ford."

"Good idea, Tom. Let me check on my men."

Adams unrolled his bedroll and moved his saddle closer to the fire. *I'm not Kit Carson*, he thought. *I'll just grab a couple of hours by the fire.*

Adams rolled up in his bedroll and gazed at the clear night sky. The Army bivouac was settling in, and the sound of the horses snorting and men securing their gear in the night air was comforting to him.

I've really gone soft, he thought. *Sleeping on the trail is more discomfort than I remember.*

It seemed to Adams that only a few minutes had passed when he was awakened by the clatter and movement of men and horses. Orienting himself, he looked around, then remembered that he was on the trail with the cavalry in pursuit of the renegade Indian band that had murdered John Reed and abducted Reed's wife and infant child. He quickly arose, made up the bedroll, and saddled up his horse.

It was 0200 hours, he guessed, and they were about to move out across Forty Mile Desert.

"Mornin', Tom. Bright-eyed and bushy-tailed, are we?"

"Morning, Jeb. I'd be a little brighter with some coffee in me, but I'll have to do without this morning. Find any trail in the desert?"

"Three of 'em. Looks like White Feather split up into three groups to throw off anyone that were followin' him. My guess is that the three regrouped just before Pyramid Lake, then moved up and made camp by the lake for a couple o' days to rest up and hunt for food for the rest of the trip north. I reckon that if we push on, we'll be only 'bout a day or so behind 'em. They'll be movin' slow-like 'cause they figure that we're lookin' for 'em to the south."

"Good. We better tell the major."

"Already have. We'll cross followin' the north-most track and rest the horses on the other side. I should be able to pick up the whole party somewhere over there."

"Mount up, Cap'n. We're movin' out."

"Right, Jeb. Ready to go."

The cavalry company had formed the column of twos and was ready to move when Adams and Ford rode up. Major Twitchell was mounted and ready.

"Morning, men. Ready to ride?"

"Morning, Major. Jeb rousted me, and I'm ready to go."

The major raised his right arm, waited until he was sure that the first sergeant had seen him, then dropped it to his side in the time-honored cavalry signal to move out.

The men moved out onto the desert at a lope. If the pace could be maintained, the desert would be left behind just before sunrise. could

The moonlight bathed the barren landscape in an eerie ghostly glow. Adams could see nothing but hard-packed sand and scrabble. Off in the distant northwest horizon, the Sierra Nevadas presided majestically over the Godforsaken fallow panorama.

"Never seen anything quite like it, Tom?"

"Never have, Jeb. Gives me the willies. There is an aura of death here. I can sense it."

"Well, I don't know 'bout what aura means, but if it was daylight, you wouldn't have to ride very far before seein' bleached bones of men and livestock that tried movin' across too slow without water. Sandstorms can whip up the sandy top sudden-like and cause a man to lose his direction.

"No, sir, Tom, night crossin's the safest way to get across."

"Well, I, for one, will be glad to get this stretch behind us."

"Ain't too many here this mornin' would take issue with you on that. Reckon another hour 'n a half or two and we can pull up to let the Army rest its horses."

"You said the Army, Jeb. That mean we're not?"

"Well, I've got to pick up the trail from there. You can rest if you need to."

The mountain man's barb was not lost on Tom Adams.

"Tell you what, old-timer. If you can keep going, so can I."

"Alright, Tom. I can use another set of eyes."

The night ride passed quickly, and the desert boundary was reached just before sunrise. The company halted for some rest and feed for the horses and a trail breakfast for the soldiers. As Pyramid Lake was nearby, it was deemed unwise to light a fire. The company would remain there for two hours and, depending on the result of Jeb Ford's tracking, would likely continue the hunt for the renegades.

Before leaving, Jeb Ford met with Adams and the Army officers and noncoms in an informal briefing.

"I want to let you all know what to expect up ahead," he told them. "'Bout an hour's ride from here is the Northern Paiute reservation. They'll be 'bout two thousand 'r more Paiutes there, but they are at peace with the white man since the 1860 Paiute wars here, and my guess is that they'll shun Al White Feather 'cause they ain't lookin' for a rematch.

I expect that he'll try and hide there but the tribal elders will let him and his renegades fish there for a day or two and then send him and anyone who wants to go with him on they way north.

"White Feather won't like bein' turned away, but he's bad medicine for the tribes there, and they'll have none of his shenanigans, so I expect he'll be there a day, two at most, and then head out with them that want to throw in with him. He may leave with more warriors than he got there with or mebbe less, just don't know.

"I do know that he ain't worried 'bout bein' tracked or he'd be a sight more careful than he has been, so that's in our favor.

"I'll be back in an hour or so with a better grip on what's ahead. Tom, I'd like you to ride out with me."

"Consider it done, Jeb."

"Good. Major, I'd like a couple of your best trail men to ride out with us if that is okay with you."

"Certainly, Mr. Ford. Sergeant Mulhauser, who do you have for this mission?"

"I'd like to go myself, Major. Sergeant Enyeart can act in my absence, and Corporal Crews is an old Injun hand."

"Very well. Make it so." Twitchell turned and spoke to Ford.

"One question. What do you suggest we do if the Paiutes don't kick White Feather out?"

Jeb Ford looked at Major Twitchell and, grinning broadly, replied,

"Go down there in your column of twos with you at the head and tell 'em that we're the advance party of a full regiment of blue bellies that ain't a day behind and that we come for Al White Feather and if they don't turn him over, we'll make bad medicine for the whole tribe."

Major Twitchell stared at Ford in disbelief.

"And you think that will actually work?"

Still grinning, Jeb Ford replied,

"Won't know 'til we try. Alright, boys, let's move out."

The four men mounted their horses and had begun to leave the company when Jeb Ford signaled for a halt in order to brief the scout party.

"We'll skirt around to the east of the lake. We'll be looking for the track of a large party, maybe twenty or thirty. Track'll be no more'n two days old, I reckon. Hoof prints, horse apples, bent grass, anything that might give us an idea of White Feather's direction."

Mulhauser addressed a question to Ford.

"We headin' east 'cause you think they headin' for Bannock tribal land up northeast?"

"Right. Let's move out."

The four men split up, searching the eastern rim of the lake without success. Any track that Al White Feather's band might have left was obscured within the many tracks of animals that came to drink the brackish lake water and the Paiute hunting parties that stalked them. After an hour, Jeb called the trackers together.

"Any luck on pickin' up White Feather's trail?" he asked.

Mulhauser spoke for the two soldiers.

"Too much damn traffic along the trail from the Paiutes. Cain't be sure."

Jeb hadn't any luck in picking up a trail as well.

"Yep. Not much along the back scrub, either. Let's get on back."

The four trackers wheeled about and headed for the main body of soldiers. Upon reaching the main column Ford rode up to give Major Twitchell the report of the trackers' lack of success.

"Have you had any luck picking up the renegade trail, Mr. Ford?"

"Afraid not, Major. Too many tracks to tell who's who. I think we'll have to go and smoke with the elders on that Paiute reservation."

"Do you think that White Feather and his band are still hiding there?"

"Possibly, but if they are, the Paiutes won't fuss 'bout givin' them up. They'd be bad medicine for the tribe if they wouldn't give them up."

Mulhauser spoke up.

"I reckon they mebbe gave 'em a day or so and then told 'em to hit the trail. These Paiutes don't want another war with the Army."

Ford nodded in asssent.

"Yep. I agree, but we'll need to know which way they was headed for certain, and they's only one way to find out, and that'll be down there on that Paiute reservation.

"Now Major, this is your show, but you have brought me along to help out with tracking and such. I've been around these Northern Paiutes a long time, and I can tell you the best way for us to handle it if you want to listen."

Major Twitchell nodded and said,

"I'm for rolling down there and letting the Paiutes know who's in charge here and by God they'd better turn this renegade over to the Army or there'll be pure Hell to pay."

"Well, we can do that, and if that's what you say, then that's what we'll do, but I'd like to suggest a way that we can get what we want and still keep our hair."

Adams broke in with a comment.

"We'd be outmanned more'n thirty to one down there. Might run out of bullets before it was over and done with."

Ford offered a counter strategy:

"Let me make a suggestion that maybe will let us stay alive down there. While the Paiute is at peace with us, they are still a proud people who, if need be, are very formidable warriors. If we cause them to lose face, we'll never get out of there alive.

"I reckon we ought to ride down to within four hunnert yards or so from the reservation, makin' all the racket we can, then stop there, and three or four of us go into camp and talk with the tribe *po-hi-na-vi*."

The major gave Ford a puzzled look.

"Who?"

"The chief. We pay our respects to him and tell him that you, the white *po-hi-na-vi*, have many blue bellies with you, with more on the way and that you are lookin' for White Feather, who has murdered and raped white women and children, thereby causin' great harm and distrust. You wish to take White Feather back for the white man's justice and if he is here, they should give him up and avoid bad medicine between the white man's army and the Paiute.

"I have had many years of talkin' with Northern Paiutes, and I will do the talkin'. You just sit there with the look of a white *po-hi-na-vi* and just nod when I turn and look at you. This will give you status with the chief and his elders."

Twitchell turned to his first sergeant and spoke.

"Sergeant, you have been out here for a number of years. What is your opinion?"

"I was up to my ears in the sixty war with these redskins, and I'll tell you they gave as good as they got."

Removing his hat to reveal a balding head, he continued,

"While I ain't got all that much to lose, I'd sure like to keep what's left."

The first sergeant continued.

"Major, I think we ought to listen to Jeb and see cain't we accomplish our mission without gettin' ourselves into a scrape with them redskins down there."

Twitchell pondered his sergeant's words for a bit, then laughed and spoke.

"Well, Sergeant, I'd hate to think that I was the one who cost you your hair. We'll try Mr. Ford's idea, but be sure that you have the company ready to move at the first sign of trouble."

Grinning from ear to ear, the first shirt responded to Major Twitchell s order.

"Yes, sir!

"Sergeant Enyeart! Mount the company and form a column of twos. Ready to move out on command!"

"Aye, First Sergeant."

As the company was forming to ride to the new bivouac site near the Paiute reservation, Adams turned to Ford and spoke sotto voce.

"For a minute there, I thought that damn major was going to get us all killed."

"Yep. I'll say one thing 'bout our shiny new major, he's a quick study. Knows when to listen to folks who know the lay of the land."

"Yes, thank God. Have to give him that."

Formed up and on the move, the soldiers reached the new site within an hour. Major Twitchell halted the columns and gave the order to dismount. He then rode over to Ford and Adams, who were on the company point, studying the Paiute reservation several hundred yards distant.

"Well, Mr. Ford, whom do you recommend go down there with me?"

"The three of us and maybe Mulhauser. He looks weathered and beat-up enough to convince them that there are some pretty tough horse soldiers with us."

"Done. I'm sure my first sergeant will appreciate your description.
Sergeant Mulhauser!"

"Sir!"

"Front and center!"

"Sir!"

The first shirt rode up at a gallop to join the major and the two Wells Fargo men on the point.

The major addressed him. "Mr. Ford has requested that you ride down with us to meet the reservation elders, and I have agreed. He says that your appearance will no doubt convince the tribe that we have some old-hand Indian fighters in our midst."

"That so, Major? Well, Jeb, I don't see no goddam blue ribbons hangin' on you, neither."

Jeb Ford grinned.

"True. Major, when do you want to ride in?"

"Might as well get it over with. I'll rely on your judgment with these redskins."

"Alright. We ride in tall and slow and ride toward the reservation center. I'm sure that by the time we get there, the elders will be waitin' for us. One of the elders prob'ly speaks some English, and I can speak a little Paiute, so we'll get our message across to 'em."

With the plan explained, Jeb said, "Let's git goin'. Me and the major up front, and Tom, you and the sergeant follow. We ride in slow, as slow as we kin. That shows 'em we ain't lookin' for no trouble."

Adams, the former Army captain, turned to Mulhauser and asked,

"Do we need a white flag or anything?"

"No, we ain't at war with 'em. Relax and show you ain't nervous."

With a nod of his head, the major gave the signal to move slowly toward the Indian reservation, and they reached the reservation perimeter within fifteen minutes. Waiting for them were several hundred Paiute men, women, and children all staring at the four white men as if they were some rarely seen oddity, which they probably were. It had been years since the Army had operated in the Pyramid Lake sector.

As the men proceeded into the reservation, the throng of curious onlookers parted as if the crowd were water parting over a ship's bow, then closing behind the four riders and following in their wake. Upon arriving in the center of the reservation, they were greeted by seven older men who appeared to be the tribal elders.

Ford assumed correctly that that the elder in the center of the others was the tribal chief. Turning to Twitchell, he gave the major a quick nod and spoke.

"Give us a halt, Major."

Twitchell, playing the part he was born to, straightened himself and majestically raised his right hand for the four to halt.

Ford addressed the tribal chief.

"Greetings, *po-hi-na-vi* of the *nu-vu*."

"Greetings, *ta-vi-vo-o*."

"Does the Paiute *po-hi-na-vi* speak the tongue of the *ta-vi-vo-o*?"

The Paiute chief nodded in assent and said,

"I am who the *ta-vi-vo-o* call Has No Horse. I speak the *ta-vi-vo-o* talk. Why do the blue bellies camp near our land?"

Ford gestured toward Major Twitchell and replied,

"This is the *po-hi-na-vi* called Major who leads many horse soldiers in search of the Paiute White Feather, who has murdered and raped many *ta-vi-vo-o mo-gho-ni* and *tu-wa-nu-vi*. White Feather is bad medicine for the Paiute who shelter him and his renegades. If White Feather is hiding among you, Major wishes you to give him up peacefully."

Twitchell looked at the chief and nodded.

A look of disgust crossed Has No Horse's face. He answered,

"White Feather is Bannock! Bannock is bad medicine for the Paiute. We live here in peace and harmony with our white *wannnaga a*. The fish are plentiful and we hunt the animals who come to drink the water. White Feather is not here."

"Have the Bannock White Feather and his renegades come by here before us?"

"Two sunrises past. Bannock are kin. We tell White Feather to fish the lake for food and then leave. He is here one day and then go away with his warriors."

"Did the Bannock have *ta-vi-vo-o* captives in his war party?"

"I did not see the Bannock war party. White Feather wished to smoke with Has No Horse. He was sent away."

"Which way did White Feather take?"

"White Feather must travel to his Bannock people in the great mountains. *Poohwi!*" Has No Horse gestured toward the northeast and repeated, "*Poohwi!*"

Ford turned and spoke to Major Twitchell.

"They are a day ahead and headin' for Bannock country up in Big Sky."

The major broke his silence and queried Ford,

"Do they know that we are on their trail?"

Has No Horse, understanding the major's question to Ford, replied,

"Tell the major *po-hi-na-vi* of the blue bellies that White Feather does not know that the blue bellies follow him."

Twitchell turned and addressed Jeb.

"The fort is at half strength. We need to get after White Feather and rescue the civilians and ride back. My provost is in command with barely forty men."

Ford nodded and addressed Has No Horse.

"We thank the *nu-vu po-hi-na-vi* for his words. We must now gather our force and move to rescue the *ta-vi-vo-o* captives and return them to our fort."

"Then you must ride quickly. The *ta-vi-vo-o* captives are in great danger."

"Major, give the chief a sign of appreciation for his help, then turn us. We'll ride out slowly until we clear the reservation," Ford said.

Major Twitchell turned and addressed Has No Horse for the first time.

"We thank the great Paiute chief for his welcome. We must go now and rescue the captives."

The four riders turned and wheeled their mounts about and rode slowly back toward the reservation boundaries. When clear, they rode at a gallop toward the soldiers camped a short distance away.

Arriving at the full company, Ford, Adams, Mulhauser, and Major Twitchell held a brief council.

Ford was first to speak.

"That Paiute knows more about the women than he let on. I take that to mean that he was afraid to tell us everything."

"What do you think that means, Mr. Ford?" Twitchell asked.

The major hadn't suspected anything more than the face-value exchange between Ford and the Paiute chief.

"I expect that the captives are either dead or badly tortured."

"Well, then, gentlemen, it is time to mount up and ride. The sooner we overtake the renegades, the more chance of the captives being rescued.
Sergeant Mulhauser, prepare the men to move out."

"Right, Major. Sergeant Enyeart, mount the company and prepare to ride out."

"Aye, Top."

Jeb Ford addressed the major.

"I'll ride on ahead and see what's to be found. When we clear the lake area, the trail ought to be easier to pick up. Meantime, head the men in the general direction that the Paiute gave us. I'll be back when I can pick up White Feather's trail.
Tom, want to ride out with me?"

"I'm ready to go!" Tom replied.

The two riders left the company at a gallop and in a short period of time had put Pyramid Lake well behind them.

About an hour into the search for White Feather's track, Ford made a motion that he was going to look further east and motioned Adams to join him in the new search.

"Might be headin' up towards the West Humboldt Range. Let's have a look up that way."

The two men had ridden a short distance in the direction of the West Humboldt when Adams, riding about one hundred yards ahead of Ford, let out a yell. He had found what appeared to be the track of a travois pulled by horse. The travois had left deep ruts, which indicated that whoever had left the tracks had it in mind to make a long journey. The tracks followed a trail of unshod hoof tracks.

Ford came riding over at a gallop to see what Adams had found.

"There ya go, Cap'n," he said. "I'll bet that we've got 'em and they plan to make a long ride, which means that we'll need to find 'em tonight before the major decides to return to the fort.

Tom, can you get on back to the major and let him know we've picked up the trail and that we can more'n likely overtake 'em tonight?"

"Right. I'm on my way."

Adams turned and rode off at a gallop to meet the Army and guide them back to Ford, who continued to track the renegades' movement to the north and east.

Riding at full gallop, Adams reached Major Twitchell within the hour. Upon seeing Adams approach, Twitchell had given the signal for the company to mount up.

"We found the trail heading toward the West Humboldts," Adams explained. "They're pulling a heavy sled and moving slow. Jeb reckons we'll have 'em by late tonight or first light tomorrow. I'm to guide you up to the trail."

"There'll be plenty of time to rest our horses when we overtake the renegades," Twitchell figured. "Sergeant Mulhauser, give the signal to form twos."

"Aye, sir."

Mulhauser raised his right arm to full extension, with two fingers extended from the fist.

When the columns were formed, the major raised his right arm and brought it swiftly down to his side.

The Army was on the move.

Once the company was in full motion, Major Twitchell extended his right arm horizontally from his body, with forearm upright and hand in a fist and began pumping the fist and arm up and down rapidly, signaling the men to advance at full gallop.

Twitchell's company moved rapidly toward the rendezvous with Ford, who by now was at least two hours ahead. They were hoping to overtake him by midafternoon.

*   *   *

Time passes rather quickly at full gallop for all but the horses. The Army horses were showing signs of tiring after the first half hour. Sergeant Mulhauser rode up to the major with the report that some of the older mounts were tiring and would be lost if the pace were continued for much longer. The major, who was trained in infantry and not cavalry, was more than willing to give the order to slow to a lope, as his own hindquarters were feeling the strain of the faster pace. He was, as the first shirt was to say later, about to fall off his damned horse!

The company slowed to a loping trot for the rest of the distance and finally met up with Jeb Ford later that afternoon.

Ford briefed the major and the first sergeant, producing a patch of brightly colored cloth. The fabric and design matched the first one that they had found earlier.

"Reckon she's leavin' a trail for any who might be lookin' for her," he said.

Adams nodded.

"And she's still alive. How far ahead of us do you think they are?"

"Draggin' that travois has slowed 'em down some, and we've been movin' pretty quick. I'd say by now they'd be no more'n eight hours ahead. Leastways whoever's lookin' after that travois is."

Twitchell turned to Sergeant Mulhauser and asked a question.

"Sergeant, do you think we need to rest the horses?"

"Mebbe wipe 'em down and rest fer a half hour, Major, then head out again."

"Very well. Mr. Ford, does that suit our progress?"

"It'll have to. Cain't catch 'em on foot."

"Very well. Sergeant Mulhauser, make it so."

"Aye, sir."

The afternoon progressed in much the same fashion: ride at a lope for two hours, then rest the horses for one half hour. Just before sunset, the outline of the West Humboldt Mountains appeared in the distant horizon. The troop continued on at a slightly slower pace in the moonlit night until just before midnight, when Ford, who had been scouting ahead, returned with news of the renegades.

"White Feather's made camp for at least tonight, maybe more, 'bout an hour ahead. Looks to be 'bout forty Bannock. Didn't see any squaws with 'em and didn't see the captives.

"They are camped near the Humboldt base in a small ravine next to the river. I think we should remain here and move up to within a few hundred yards in small groups. By sunup, we'll be in place and surprise 'em."

The major was now in his element.

"Sergeant, we'll send up one squad at a time until we are in place for the attack. Mr. Ford, is there some high ground that we can occupy that will be favorable for an advance on horseback?"

"Reckon so. Problem is, if we post the horses too close, the Bannock horses might get wind and spook. Then we'd be a dead giveaway. Best you think about dismountin' and goin' in afoot."

"At last, we're talking my language. Let's keep the horses at a rear staging area, and we'll advance on foot under cover until we are in a position for the attack."

As the expedition moved slowly toward the Bannock camp, a light snowfall began, which slowed the men's progress and made the trail difficult to follow. By 0100 hours, Major Twitchell's company had halted a mile or so from the flickering light of the Bannock campfires. The renegades had apparently planned to remain at the site for several days and had put up their tipis.

"We can stop here and tie the horses to the scrub," Twitchell said. "Sergeant Mulhauser, detail three men to look after the horses. Have each man in the attack party be sure that they have a full cartridge belt and both sidearm and rifle with them when they move up. We'll advance on foot the rest of the way, one squad at a time, until we reach our position above the camp. Mr. Ford, I'd like you to lead the first two squads to the jump-off position. Once the first two squads are in place, you may send one man back to lead the next squad up, and so forth until the company is in place. I want you to remain there and position the squads in not only the best tactical position but in a position where we are likely not to be detected before the attack.

"Sergeant Mulhauser, I want you to brief your NCOs that there are white women and a child being held captive down there. Have them expend their ammunition wisely. No wild or indiscriminate shooting that may harm the hostages."

"Right, Major."

"Sergeant Enyeart, collect the NCOs for a briefing."

Ford, realizing that the Army was chewing up precious time, spoke up.

"Right. Let's get goin'. We need to move quiet-like so's not to spook any o' them Bannock ponies. We get spotted early before everybody's in place and ready, it'll be pure Hell to pay."

The snowfall helped the men move forward quietly one squad at a time without detection until the entire company of sixty was in place and waiting for the signal to attack.

Twitchell gathered up his first sergeant, Ford, Adams, and Sergeant Enyeart.

"We'll go on my hand signal at first light," he told them. "One hour before, we'll begin moving up on the camp in a belly crawl. The closer we can get without detection will maximize the element of surprise. I'll lead the charge, and each of you lead the men in your sectors. Once we are on the move, Mr. Ford suggests that we make as much noise as possible going in. That will spook the savages' horses and cause some confusion in the camp. Be on the lookout for the hostages and use your ammunition effectively. If we go in there in a coordinated attack, I expect that we should have the field before noon and the hostages safe and under our protection. Should we capture White Feather, I intend to convene a military trial on the spot."

At 0530 hours, the major gave the order to begin the belly crawl through the freezing snow toward the camp, which lay below, one hundred yards distant. The men crawled forward, repeating rifles nestled in the crooks of their elbows.

Adams, belly-crawling with the soldiers, wondered if the renegades could hear the sound of his chattering teeth.

When the company had crawled to within thirty yards of the camp, a Bannock renegade emerged from one of the tipis and walked out twenty yards or so to relieve himself. Upon pulling down his buckskin pants, he looked up to find himself within five yards of a soldier who had been crawling toward the camp. The renegade let out a yelp, pulled up his buckskins, and began to run for his tipi to get his weapon. The soldier stood erect, cocked and aimed his rifle, and shot the renegade in his exposed buttock, which generated yet another yelp from the Bannock.

Looking in the direction of the rifle shot, Twitchell realized that there was no further surprise to be sprung, jumped up, and began issuing the order to charge.

"Let's go, men! Kill the renegades! God and country!"

The initial report from the cavalryman's rifle had spooked the Bannock horses and set the camp in a state of confusion and panic. As the renegades emerged from their tipis, firing wildly, they were cut down by Major Twitchell's men. A few, unable to find their horses, ran toward the nearby river and were shot trying to flee the battle.

Tom Adams entered the tipi nearest him to find it deserted. There were articles of women's clothing and personal effects scattered about the dirt floor. *This must where the hostages were kept*, he thought, *but where are they now?*

The fight had continued for more than a half hour, and there were casualties on both sides. The Bannock had managed to overcome their initial confusion and were mounting a fierce counterattack. Many of the men were engaged in vicious hand-to-hand fighting with the renegades.

Adams, pistol drawn, exited the tipi that had held the captives and was immediately set upon by a Bannock warrior. Struggling for possession of his pistol with his adversary, Adams tripped the warrior, and the two fell to the ground, continuing to grapple for possession of his Remington. As they rolled on the ground, Adams freed his left hand, grabbed a rock that was lying in close proximity, and smashed it into the Indian's face. Stunned, the Bannock momentarily released his grip on the pistol, whereupon Adams shot him through the heart.

Adams continued to search the camp for the hostages as the fight neared its conclusion. The Army had won the day, and but for a few renegades still furiously fighting, the battle would have been finished. He entered the last tipi in the camp, and his heart sank. Lying on the floor were Carmen Reed and her infant daughter. Their throats had been cut at some point during the battle, and they had been left to bleed to death.

Carmen Reed's appearance was shocking. Emaciated and drawn, she was covered with cuts and deep bruises. It was obvious that she had been repeatedly tortured and raped. Her infant daughter bore signs of torture of the most horrible kind.

Adams sat on the dirt floor next to the bodies and wept. He had envisioned the company rescuing the woman and child and returning them safely to civilization, where they would be able to begin anew, but now this! He felt a hatred welling up inside him. He wanted to exact revenge on as many of these bloodthirsty animals as he could. He left the tent to look for the savages who had done this, with murder in his heart.

As he left the tipi, Adams saw that the battle was done. It had scarcely been an hour from beginning to end.

He felt a frustration that would be difficult to put to rest at knowing that he would not have an opportunity to exact his revenge.

Major Twitchell had received a slight head wound while fighting hand to hand with a Bannock warrior. Adams approached him with the news.

"Major, when you have finished having your wound dressed, you'd better come with me."

"Damn the wound, sir. Have you found the hostages?"

"I have. They are in the end tipi nearest the river."

"I expect they were glad to see you, sir, after being held by these savages."

"Better come with me, Major. You too, Jeb."

The three men walked to the tipi where Adams had discovered the bodies of Carmen Reed and her daughter, and they walked inside.

"Jesus, Mary, and Joseph!"
Twitchell turned abruptly and left the tipi.

"Sergeant Mulhauser, do we have an assessment of our dead and wounded?"

"Four wounded—one seriously—and four dead. Corporal Forrest was among the killed."

"We will take our men back to the fort for burial. The hostages have been murdered. Have Corporal Crews assign a burial detail to bury Mrs. Reed and her child. Bury the child with the mother."

"Yes, sir. Why aren't we carrying them back with us?"

"You may go see the remains if you wish and then answer your own question. "Sergeant, have we taken any prisoners?"

"Four, Major. They was trying to get to the river when they was caught. Two is wounded, one pretty bad."

"Bring them to me for questioning."

"Aye."

Adams and Ford approached the major, who was by now standing in the center of the Bannock camp.

"We have four prisoners. I'm going to question them," the major told them.

Mulhauser returned with the four captured Bannock. One had a wound to his right shoulder. Another was seriously wounded with a bullet in his abdomen.

"Stand 'em up in a line, Sergeant," Twitchell ordered.

Mulhauser gestured to the Bannock prisoners and formed them in a line facing the major.

"Which of you can talk the white talk?"

The prisoner with the shoulder wound replied,

"I speak the white man talk."

"Where is White Feather?"

"I do not know of this White Feather of your talk."

"You do know this White Feather. He is the leader of your renegades."

"I do not know."

Jeb addressed the major.

"That's White Feather you're talkin' to."

"What? How do you know that?"

"Nobody else would speak out of turn without the war party chief sayin' so. That's White Feather."

"Are you certain?"

"Yep."

"Sergeant Mulhauser, find a rope and a stout tree and hang this murderer. He has been found guilty by military trial."

"Aye, Major, with pleasure. What you want me to do with him when we're done?"

"Leave him hanging as a reminder to those that would entertain the idea that they can murder and rape women and children."

"Aye, sir. Corporal Rosenthal, get three men, a horse, and a rope. We's about to carry out the court's sentence." The sergeant turned back to Twitchell and asked,

"What about these other three, sir?"

"Shoot 'em."

The major, Adams and Ford turned and walked back toward the tipi where the remains of Mrs. Carmen Reed and her daughter had been found. As they walked away, three shots rang out.

"That takes care of the murdering Bannock," the major said. "We'll have the hanging in short order."

Adams turned to the major and replied,

"I'll stay to see that murdering bastard hung, then I must take leave of you and your men. I have Wells Fargo business that I must address. Will you be needing Jeb Ford's services?"

"No, I'd say not." Turning to Jeb, he said,

"Mr. Ford, your service to us has been of incalculable value. The United States Army thanks you for a job well done."

"Thanks, Major. Reckon I'll ride back with Tom, here, and get back to work."

In short order, a sturdy tree and limb were located and a rope was readied for the execution. White Feather's hands were tied behind him, and the hangman's noose was placed around his neck, then thrown over the tree limb and secured to the trunk. Two soldiers lifted the renegade into the saddle of a cavalry horse.

As major Twitchell approached the renegade Bannock, White Feather spoke.

"I wish for the white chief to shoot. I will not die in this low way."

"You are unworthy of an Army bullet, White Feather. You are a low murderer and torturer of defenseless women and children."

With that remark, Twitchell took off his hat and slapped the hindquarters of the horse, which then bolted and surged forward in a gallop. White Feather, suspended in midair by only his neck, began to kick and thrash about wildly, eyes bulging and mouth in a grotesque contortion.

After several minutes, the thrashing stopped and White Feather's legs ceased kicking. He remained hanging, twisting slowly in an odd counterclockwise motion.

Mulhauser approached the major.

"What do you want done with the dead redskins, Major?"

"Leave 'em for the coyotes, Sergeant. They are not worth our sweat.

And burn the camp down. I want nothing but ashes here."

"Aye, sir. If ye don't mind my sayin'...well...welcome to the cavalry! I'm proud to ride under yer command."

* * *